COLORADO COMRADE

MJ Politis, Ph.D.

276 5th Avenue Suite 704 #944

New York, NY 10001

Cover Design by Woodbridge Publishers.

Find out more about our upcoming releases and authors at www.woodbridgepublishers.com and sign up for our newsletter to stay updated!

Dedicated to you…the reader. With appreciation for your
being open to this offering.
And all those I have known who made this offering
possible.

CHAPTER 1

1935, Colorado

Being a creature who told time according to the sun, its position in the sky, and the duration it replaced the moon, the cow resisted being moved from the still, grassy, and greenish brown pasture in the Colorado high country to winter corals. She was ambivalent about being sent to a railroad car destined for someplace where perhaps the grass still had some green in it. She had given birth to seven calves thus far, having seen them all grow up to be parents themselves, or become passengers on the large, noisy iron horses which moved on wheels rather than legs. Perhaps her fear of the latter drove her calf to resist being moved by the cowboys who were pushing the herd down the mountain along the gentle slopes leading up to the high country. Or, perhaps, there was a fascination the calf had with the cliff overlooking the valley below. Or perhaps the calf thought he could spread his feet out and fly like the eagles in the clouds. The birds who dipped down to the river to fetch fish three times their size, or the hawks that lingered somewhat lower to fetch slow-moving rabbits. Then there were the low-flying crows that pecked out the eyes and entrails of any four-legged creature that stopped breathing, eating, and defecating.

The harder the cowboys yelled, the faster the calf ran toward the cliff, weaving in and out of brush that most horses would have to go around rather than sneak under. Indeed, the cow had no choice but to follow her calf, even if it led to the demise of both of them. The eight-year-old cow, though she had the muscle mass and strength of a one-year-old heifer, saw the world through life-tired eyes which were becoming less functional each year. As such, she knew the cowboys in weather-beaten and torn clothing riding magnificent-looking horses atop worn-out saddles, which had been yet again repaired rather than finally replaced. She recognized each of the two-legged humans on the four-legged equines by voice as much as by sight as they moved the rest of the herd along to whatever pasture or feed lot they would be sent to in the upcoming winter. A winter, according to the large amount of fur growing on her hide and the others, would be a cold one.

There was Jake Hanson, hotheaded, loud-mouthed 25 25-year-old crude cowboy. The fuzz on his upper lip never really grew thick enough to be a real man's mustache. He appended most of his yells at the cow's fellow bovines with the crack of his whip, a spit on the ground, or an expletive of frustration, or all three. The horse between his oversized spurs seemed as unwilling to move as any of the cattle.

Riding on the other side of the herd was freckle-faced Buddy Emerson, whose horse did most of what he asked of it. He was usually a quiet cowhand who did everything Jake said to do, including yelling at the cattle and his horse, when he didn't have to.

Riding drag behind the defiant young and life-tired older cattle who wanted to stay atop the grassy pasture that would become an ice covered, slippery skating rink or buried under three feet of snow within the next week, was their boss, Sam Longmore, At the end of this particularly dry summer, his skin was deep red, his hair completely white now. His mustache had grown over his lower lip and nearly his chin. The wrinkles on his face were deeper this year than the last, for reasons he never told Jake or Buddy. Sam seemed to confide a common fate of doom with any cow he looked at. In a herd, he worked harder each year to keep. A herd that ate better than he did, by the looks of his slender belly and gaunt face. But there was the hope that better days were ahead, particularly during the middle of what he called The Great Depression. So he kept promising everything walking on two or four legs around him.

On this day, the cow, known to the humans (and only them) as 127, was more concerned about her runaway calf, labeled as 127K. That new arrival into the world was ignored by the rest of the cows, who were under the spell of the bull in front of the herd, or the mounted humans pushing them. For now, anyway. It was a situation that could change at any time if the calf, or she, led them astray, to the overlook where more than one calf, cow, or bull had fallen to its death.

Dashing out to help her, the calf, and eventually the herd was a cowhand about the same age as Jake, biologically anyway, by the name of Kumar Patel. His skin seemed to be not as white as the other cowhands and not as black as the Colored cowboys Sam hired in the 'good old' days before the Depression. He ran his horse, a comrade rather than master to the equine beast he called 'Arjun', towards the calf, and the cow, cutting both off from near falls down the cliff no less than three times. He sang his requests to the calf to move back up to the rest of the herd in a strange language that seemed to the mother cow as Ancient and kind, rather than yelling at her and her precocious son with harsh orders in English. Or Lakota.

The cow didn't know what the words in Kumar's song meant, but whatever they were, it worked. Kumar and his horse, both of whom were very much liked when looked at by the ladies in town (the red-skinned and the white ones), were able to convince 127's calf to join his mother, then the herd. Such saved both of them from falling over the cliff. And stumbling in holes made in the ground that broke the legs of two other cows. And preventing the cow and calf from taking a drink from a pool of water that smelled 'off'. And a slow, agonizing death befell the cows, calves, and bulls whose skulls were scattered around the once safe and now toxic pond.

Cow 127 moo'd a thank you to Kumar, which he responded to with a bow of his head. He then got back to his position with Sam in the back of the, thankfully, not stampeding herd.

"Great job," Sam said to Kumar with a thumbs-up up shown to him only.

Kumar replied in a language that Sam didn't understand. The old man raised his eyebrows to the young one with concern and curiosity.

"Hindi for 'no problem,'" Kumar answered with a warm smile, and an accent which was as American as any of the other cowboys, but far more literate and seemingly refined. "Loosely translated," he continued with the wisdom of an old man in a young one's body, hiding a wealth of secrets behind his deep, thinking brown eyes.

Interrupting Kumar's thinking, just before he seemed to confide something to Sam, was none other than Jake. "Big time problem if he talks that East Indian gibberish in town again," Jake shot back from a mouth as ugly as his tone, after which he spat on the ground.

"HIS problem, not ours," Sam said to the fifth-generation White skinned American spoiled brat he felt obligated to hire on. Who was orphaned after Sam's best friend died of the Spanish flu ten years ago? "Or YOURS."

"Sure," Jake grumbled back to Sam, as Kumar ran off to sing a Hindi request to American-raised cattle. "But Kumar reckons these cows are incarnations of really great people. Which means---"

"----That you should take care of them like they are," Sam shot back at Jake's resentful and jealous face. After which Sam rode back to his position in the herd, Jake taking his place after an angry sigh.

The cattle drive progressed further down the mountain, the ground having less edible growth on it with each loss of elevation. The bits of dirt churned up by the bull and his harem of heifers in the lead turned into clouds of dry dust, which made the cattle, horses, and cowboys cough.

Ironically, the river for which Blue River was named still flowed behind the dusty fields. Those once lush fields that supported grass for cows and crops for people were now hard slabs of dirt that sprouted pockets of inedible and toxic weeds. Cow 127, or as Kumar secretly named her, Indira, recognized one of her sisters and two of her offspring by their faces and eyes behind the mangled fences. As for the bodies connected to them, they were more bone than muscle, their feet pillars of rotting flesh. They bellowed calls for help, asking to be invited back into the herd, they were sold out, or a bullet from one of the cowboys they seemed to recognize.

In front of the broken-down pen where those once healthy cattle were was a sign reading 'Property of Morgan-Richter Financial Group'. Behind the pen lay three farm houses with boards hammered across the doors and windows. At the gate of the farm, reinforced by three layers of barbed wire, was a metal mini billboard reading 'Property of Morgan-Richter Bank. Trespassers will be shot, even if they are former owners.'

How and why the three bovines remained there and why they were permitted to remain in their condition was something Indira didn't know. But the owners of the spread, Larry Jackson, his wife, and three dirt-covered barefoot kids, were just as emaciated as the cattle they had once owned. Cow 127 saw them living in tents outside of the property with 'Will Work for Food' on the 'doorstep.'

Most of the smaller farms and the houses of people who worked in town on the trail to town were also boarded up, property of the Morgan-Richter Bank. The sun baked the land around them. Just last season, they all had been irrigated into sprouting crops for two-legged creatures and grass for those able to get around on four limbs. Ironically, the river still flowed, filling the air with a musical murmur. But the player of that watery tune was not matched with the usual harmony of farm animals enjoying being fed, or telling each other how well they had trained the two-legged humanoid mammals to feed them.

The ground under Indira's feet felt…violated somehow. Through her various senses, some of which perhaps were remnants of being a highly advanced yogi in Kumar Patel's native country during the last lifetime, she could feel the ghosts of animals from past eras under her feet. Their remains had been converted to crude oil and coal. Those 'resources' had been and even more so now were brutally pulled out of the ground in the dirtiest way possible, for the purpose of serving the wants of the rich rather than the needs of the poor.

Then there were the logged-out slopes of the mountains that echoed the dirge of sorrow and despair, holes blown into them by explosives to dig out privately owned mines, which were abandoned or boarded up. The sky felt more black than blue, but still yielded no rain, despite the efforts of those who put up signs saying 'Will Make It Rain for Food.' Those signs were appended by correcting 'make' with 'try to make' and 'food' with 'whatever you can spare'.

Indeed, Mother Nature was extracting her vengeance on the pale-skinned two-legged creatures who had, out of desperation or ignorance, taken more than they gave back. Of course, just as experienced cattle said to less learned members of their species, there was an 'I told you so' built into this. "Your Dust Bowl, not ours," the Lakota Band, who refused to join those who made the land bleed by plowing so much of it, said in a sign which was still up, despite bullet holes shot into it.

Upon entering the official town of Blue Water, Indira and her fellow bovines were herded down a street lined with boarded-up, repossessed, or abandoned wooden and brick shops, which outnumbered those still opened for business. Citizens clad in torn, mismatched clothing walked about, rummaging through the garbage cans and alleys for whatever could be used for shelter, food, or coverings for their thin arms and legs.

Behind the one and two-story structures that had been functional businesses last year were three, three and four-story dwellings made of material that was made of something else. Something shiny. Something that said the people who lived and worked in them were important. A small number of people inside and around them wore clothes that were color coordinated, which fit their plump torsos well, and with no tears or holes in them. Their bellies were fat. Their chins were raised up high. Their eyes were diverted when passing by, and insulting those not of their caste, or class, whose clothing was three sizes too large for their thin bodies.

But of more concern for Indira was what she saw in Sam's face when he looked at the sign on the coral where she was heading, as the manager of the coral approached him. Indira knew that the natural way of things was that old and sick fellow members of her bovine species were destined to be taken onto the iron horse to somewhere else, along with those who had lost the ability to produce offspring. A better place, she intuited. A chance at a new lifetime, according to what Kumar had assured them. But as for what Indira and she were worth this lifetime in her present life form, that was disappointing to Sam and insulting to her. Cattle and horse prices were half of what they were last year. But Sam, who was determined to hold onto what was left of his herd, had no choice. Indira was to be sold for the lowest price imaginable.

While being loaded onto the railroad cars, with her calf, the Cow 127 mooed a thank you to Kumar. With his eyes, from a distance, he wished her a fond farewell in his Native tongue. Promising her to carry on the lessons she had taught her.

CHAPTER 2

Feeling himself to be the eyes, ears, and, if he could figure out how, the hope of the mass of well-intending four and two-legged Coloradans, Kumar viewed what had happened in the town he had last seen two months and three baths in the cold river ago. From atop of the horse that still miraculously didn't have to sell for food and minimal lodging, the East Indian cowboy noted once prominent citizens who spent the work day at their labors milling around the streets in front of the shops which were not yet out of business or bought by Morgan and Richter management, and their other associates. So as to avoid being arrested for vagrancy, which carried a penalty of thirty dollars and as many days in jail, those lower caste citizens redistributed dust, garbage, and manure, pretending to be useful to the National Guard soldiers now wearing deputy badges.

Kumar's horse stare, then his, was held captive by a small-framed man in a weather-beaten duster, one tear away from becoming rags. Under such was an old, well-tailored suit. He lifted up his more flop than form wide-brimmed hat, wiping the sweat off his brow, then quickly placed it back on his balding head, giving Kumar a view of his face. Behind him was a tent, not unlike those used by the numerous migrants and displaced Coloradans who had lost their homes, but not yet their determination to live in dignity and honor in better times. What the fat cat upper-ups, including the new President in Washington, kept promising was just around the corner. A closer look at the assertive and watchful forty-going-on-sixty sleep-deprived gentleman who seemed more at home in a library than the real world described by books revealed that it was indeed Doc Bill Wilson.

When the soldier-deputies weren't looking, the old fart small town Doctor who liberated himself from being a prestigious (and therefore underutilized) physician in Philadelphia motioned for Mary Steiner an her eleven year old daughter Elsa to enter his tent. For a 'Bible reading', as advertised on his 'Bible Readings and Prayers for Departed Loved Ones' sign on his tent. Mary, who read the Bible, which she never believed, coughed up phlegm tinged with blood. As did Elsa when Doc Wilson listened to her heart and lungs with his stethoscope. He snuck a pouch of pills to Mary, placing them discreetly into the only intact pocket in her dress. "One a day for our literary genius, and two, twice a day for you, for a week. Just between us, or I'll be…"

The frail but certainly not afraid of the flu, or death, Elsa hugged Wilson with gratitude.

"I can't pay you, Doc," Mary said.

"Elsa just did, and will continue to do so by writing about what's happening for when the world is ready to be told about it," Doc Wilson replied, after which he took the Bible out of Mary's hands. He flashed a sign outside his tent, reading "Next", visible only to the 'commoner' in the street. The next vagrant citizen snuck into the tent, after which Doc Wilson closed the flap.

The clanking of spoons against empty metal bowls near the medical tent drew Arjun's and then Kumar's attention next. It wasn't the first time that Kumar had seen a soup line for former food providers displaced from their homes and livelihood due to wheat, corn and barley prices in New York and Chicago dropping down to almost nothing by executives who still ate high on the hog at the restaurants across the street from the still somehow intact Stock Market buildings. The soup of the day was vegetable beef, though which kind of vegetable and what kind of meat it really was remained unadvertised and unspoken about in the line of 'al fresco diners.' Some of them had lost fingers and arms in 'industrial' accidents, and had relatives who died without leaving enough money to pay for proper funeral arrangements.

Serving sandwiches, soup, and, most importantly, a double portion of dignity to every man, woman, and child on the line was Father Paul Smith. He was a middle-aged, dark-haired, blue-eyed, handsome Catholic priest, good-looking enough to be marryable to anyone in town. The naturally-dramatic Padre also had the kind of face and torso which would make him hirable as the leading man in any 'talkie' movies coming out of the Edison movie studios in New Jersey, or the emerging competitors who actually filmed Westerns in the 'paradise' most people knew as California.

Father Paul, as he preferred to be called, was beloved by Protestant vagrant Christians as well as those who forfeited their belief in the Merciful Almighty several repossessions ago. In part, this was because he dared to say that the Pope was not infallible. But more importantly, and punishable by his superiors, Father Paul encouraged fellow Catholics to read the Bible for themselves rather than insist that they only hear or are given the passages the Priests deemed appropriate. Like every other citizen of Blue River who came there by choice as an adult rather than those welcomed or cajoled out of the womb when there, Father Paul had his secrets about what kind of man he was that he dared not confess to any man. Except to Kumar in a theoretical discussion about the special qualities of the East Indian half-man, half-woman Deity, Bahuchara Mata.

Assisting Father Smith in dispensing food at the outdoor soup kitchen was Leona Thundercloud. She was attractive presumably full blooded Lakota, whose physique defined maximally attainable feminine beauty by any mortal according to Paleskin, Redskin and even brown-skin East Indian standards. With his keen sense of hearing, Kumar eavesdropped on yet another one of the typical conversations at the soup line.

Father Smith offered a meal for five to Leonard Meeker, an out of work half-breed, short haired Blackfoot, reluctantly there at the insistence of his wife and two malnourished kids behind him. His badly cropped hair made him look both diseased in the body and head. Leonard refused to take the plates offered to him by Smith. Just as Leonard was about to pull himself and his family away from the soup and sandwich line, Leona then whispered assurances to the former hunter who had forfeited his braids and dignity to get a job that paid real money in town, She informed Leonard that the bologna sandwiches were made of a mixture of moose meat from the hills and body parts from bologna-speaking fat cat White Capitalists in the East who finally came down with 'industrial accidents.' Leonard smiled with delight, finally accepting the meal for 6 delivered to the family of four.

Father Paul pro-actively short-circuited an argument from a not-yet-emaciated family of White folks behind the Red-skinned Meeker's clan, declaring that Jesus said that the primary commandment of everyone of all races is to give according to their abilities, and take according to their needs. Such was a quote that Kumar recognized from Das Capital more than any New Testament reading he had done while self-educating himself politically and philosophically. But more important than trying to find proof of that Marxist ideal in Jesus' teachings, the master East Indian cowboy and aspiring, yet not very accomplished, Labor Union organizer decided to allow himself to be fed by Leona's smile, which was directed at him. He smiled a 'hello' back, hoping, admittedly selfishly, that during his absence she hadn't found anyone else more worthy of her hand in the Comradeship of Marriage than himself.

Kumar allowed himself to think about what life would be like when he could come home to Leona's smile every day after a day of hard, honest, and, ideally anyway, service rather than profit-oriented labor. But midway through the first day's imagination, a voice from the real world, from a real boss, interrupted him.

"Eyes on the herd, son," Sam, still on his horse, said to Kumar, pointing his favorite cowhand's attention to the rest of the herd he was charged with moving into the coral for transport. "Eyes not on something bigger than we can stop," the wise old man who had survived bad business deals with those more clever, cruel, and often younger than he was said regarding the legally allowed, for now anyway, soup line, and the illegal free medical clinic. "You gotta eat, and so does that horse or yours, while you still have him."

Sam snuck a small roll of greenback Presidential portraits into Kumar's pocket. "What can I pay you, now anyway. Maybe later. When cattle, wheat, and grain prices stop hightailing it down into outhouse crapper," he related with apologetic eyes, as if all of it was his fault.. "Which they will! After all, this IS America!" the veteran of the Great War and some others he didn't talk about declared with patriotic fervor and commitment.

Kumar looked at the money, assessing quickly that it was less than he expected, or needed, to get through the winter with any degree of comfort. "It's okay," he assured Sam. "You can be rich in Creative Vision or flush in pocket, as we both know."

"And as the Lord said," Sam added, with the deepest of convictions. "A rich man has as much of a chance of gettin' into heaven as a camel does getting through the eye or a needle," he pontificated as a servant of the Almighty above.

"Unless he's got a great New York Jewboy lawyer. So I've heard. From broke Jewish comics on the radio anyway," Sam continued as a born and bred Coloradan who had seen so much of the world on the other side of the Ocean with his eyes, but not his Mind or soul.

With that, Sam rode on to manage the transport of the rest of the herd, assisted, finally, by Buddy. Kumar looked at the money stuffed into his pocket, then pulled it out. He yelled out to Leona, then pointed to the money, then her, as if to give it to her. She pointed to the collection box next to her, then smiled at him. Kumar crunched the money up in a ball and threw it to to Leona. She caught it, put it into the collection box, and then tended to her duties. She gave Kumar a Comrade to Comrade (or perhaps something more personal than that) wink. He retained it until she finished counting the money thrown to her. Before Kumar could reply in word, action, or ocular telepathy, Leona's warm smile turned into a hateful, condescending grimace. Noting the angle of her stare, it was directed to someone else, this time anyway.

"Kumar," Jake said, having ridden behind him and spitting another wad of chewing tobacco onto the ground. "Remember what Leona did to you in the last

incarnation," he said by way of ridicule of the dream Kumar related to Jake when he thought that he had a heart that felt emotion as well as pumped 'real American' blood through his cold veins. "And what she did to me in this one when I went ta her shop for a trim and a shave!" he barked at Leona. He took off his hat, revealing a bad haircut that looked more like a scalping. "When I was just tryin' to be polite to that redskin squaw," he proclaimed to any fellow Paleface who would listen, which they did. He turned again to Leona. "All I said was 'you people would make more civilized wampum if ya didn't look like and smell like wild animals.'"

Leona let Jake's comment incubate behind her thinking eyes and in her, by White, Native, and even East Indian standards, highly developed brain box. She considered the explanation for the racial slur, pulled the edges of her lips back, stroked her chin, then looked up at Jake with another blast of vengeful fire out of her oculars. She gave him a third finger salute to be sure that there was no mistaking her feelings and thoughts on the matter.

Jake put his hat on and rode on. Meanwhile, Kumar, this time before Arjun, heard a stage pull in at the other end of town in front of a newly complete ritzy four-story building. It bore a sign reading 'Blue River Deluxe Gentleman's Club, Hotel and Restaurant'. The newly erected building stood proudly next to the now boarded-up one-and-a-half-story "Workers Rights Union Hall", a sign on the door reading 'Property of Morgan-Richter Realtors.' Portions of the Worker's meeting hall were being torn down, and, by the looks of it, had been used as part of the construction for the upscale establishment, which now dwarfed it. In front of the Gentleman's club was someone who was hardly a gentleman according to truly civilized standards.

Emerson Morgan had become even more fascist, fat, fashion-conscious, and fifty over the summer than even

Kumar imagined possible. But then again, such was a requirement for the man who claimed to have rebuilt Blue River and most of Colorado during the 1920s, then was saving it from Anarchists at home and the Red Scare abroad in the 30s. Morgan was decked out in what had to be a $200 suit with, as required by business protocol, diamond cufflinks. All of it was shown off with a chin that was always upturned and never covered with any stubble or dirt, even on the dustiest day. He welcomed new members of his ruling caste to Blue River for a special power lunch after having been dropped off by the shiniest and biggest luxury cars Kumar had ever seen in person while growing up under his rich-in-pocket but poor-in-spirit and heart father in California. Or in the magazines he had read as a boy afraid to leave home, and wiped his ass with after he left California as an independent, self-liberated man.

All of the honored guests were, of course, men. They ruled most of Wyoming, Colorado, and even Utah. Most had at least three initials before their Christian name. All of them had women with them who were more beautiful on the outside than on the inside. Their male 'protectors' agreed to be relieved of that female company before entering the pre-lunch meeting room.

By Morgan's side was none other than his apprentice in 1932, assistant in 1934, \and now his associate. Russell T. Richter was younger, leaner, and had far more hair than exposed scalp on top of his head than his former mentor. By Richter's side, Mellissa Bullock, Richter's latest fiancée. She was a statuesque and beautiful 25-year-old woman of high breeding who claimed, and could verify when required to, a pedigree going back to English Monarch Queen Elizabeth I on the other side of the Atlantic. She also claimed, and so often over-proved, roots to Colonial American financial empires in Virginia and both Carolinas that somehow grew even richer after the South lost the War of Northern Aggression back in 1865.

In the competition for economic superiority, which was America's favorite pastime, Morgan had, usually legally, taken less from Kumar than from most of the citizenry of Blue River. But such made Kumar hate the balding mogul with a slick comb-over that never went out of place, even in the harshest wind, even more. Kumar's daydream about taking Morgan down economically one day, this lifetime or the next, was interrupted by a scream of pain from Doc Wilson's 'Bible Reading and Prayers for the Departed' tent. It came from an overly muscled six-foot-two patient of Doc Wilson's, who Kumar knew as a man who had as high a threshold for physical pain without screaming as Kumar had for heartbreak.

"Another 'accident' when working at the coal mine for even less than we were getting last week," Calvin DuBois said between black lung coughs.. He gritted his still mostly intact white teeth, and his face was black with coal dust. Doc Wilson continued to maneuver his injured and hopefully not permanently useless left arm. "Happened when I started talking Union to someone who I thought was one of us, Doc, but who---"

"----Rest that arm for ten days or lose it for a lifetime," Wilson interjected. He wrapped a bandage around the twisted limb, neglecting to make any attempt to close the cloth tent 'door' that DuBois had ripped apart while his arm was being pushed back into its socket.

"I'd like to oblige, Doc, but I've got work this week. Paying work," replied the underpaid miner who had sworn an oath to the mountain he had grown up on five long years ago to never 'stab in the back'. Or to 'drill holes into its soul' for the well-being of the mountain as well as the health of the people on or under it. "Who's gonna feed my family? And the twins that are on the way, despite and me wife trying to be careful? Or her not being careful with someone else behind my---" Back pain held back the rest of his frustrations and explanations.

As for doing what he could about DuBois' crisis of finances and conscience, Wilson took money out of his trouser pocket. He stuffed it into Dubois' breast pocket as discreetly as he could, but apparently not discreetly enough.

"Doctor Wilson!" Wilson and Kumar heard from Morgan. Who apparently was rudely interrupted in his imagination about how he would become richer and more powerful than the guests he was inviting to a power lunch by working with them. And, no doubt richer and more powerful still when he brought down their organizations from within. Richter and Mellissa welcomed in the moguls of the cattle, oil, coal, railroad, automobile, and soon-to-be corporatized agricultural industries into the power lunch.

"Enabling the lazy, stupid, ungrateful, and, because of such, poor, is bad business. Especially for a physician who is running low on pharmaceuticals," Morgan informed Doc, not caring who was eavesdropping on the declaration, and warning. "Doctor Wilson, no, Bill. You are welcomed to lunch, with people who can remedy that situation and your constant need for better surgical supplies," Morgan proclaimed with an open arm and welcoming smile.

Realizing Wilson was caught in a dilemma, Dubois gave back the money Doc had given him with his still-operative arm. "It's ok. Doc. You gotta do what you gotta do," the underpaid and endangered laborer said to the Philadelphia-raised scholar. While Dubois hobbled away, Wilson was still conflicted. He gazed at the patients in line for the kind of care he was becoming unable to give them with the meager supplies he had at hand.

"Doctor Wilson?" Morgan yelled across the street. "A better medical and personal

destiny awaits you." Gazing at the next set of patients ready to be seen and treated by whatever drugs Wilson still had on hand, Morgan continued. "A better destiny awaits even those people who are about to be arrested for loitering, if you…".

Wilson shed his poor man's coat, revealing a business suit under it. He shrugged his shoulder in an "I can't do any more" to the patients, then left to join Morgan et al, who welcomed him to a 'magnificent and profitable lunch' at the Gentleman's Club. Morgan shut the door behind him.

Kumar had experienced this before, but finally the prophetic words he had heard from so many old farts were about it sunk in. "Render unto Caesar that which is Caesar's," he commented to his horse Arjun. He was angry at the rich fat cats but pitied Wilson for joining them, for now anyway. "But render unto God that which is God's!" he yelled up to the Jesus spirit that was supposed to come around whenever you quoted or thought about that Visionary, Prophet, and/or Avatar, depending on your inner and outer needs at the time. "God, who's still on a lunch break, while this town goes even further into—"

Once again, Kumar's youthful wisecrack, fueled by a weird sense of Ancient wisdom willed to him by his Grandfather on his deathbed, was interrupted by even more signs in town describing who Blue River could belong to, or be served by. Above every 'help wanted' sign posted on a row of newly built offices and stores bearing Morgan or Richter's name in some way was, in even more official font--- "No Okies, Italians, Irish, Jews, Negroes, Indians or non-Coloradans need apply."

Kumar then dared to look at the Blue River Workers' Union Meeting hall, having heard hammering nails and a chainsaw from its direction that spooked Arjun. Soldiers in spotless Mountie hats and crease-pressed trousers put up a new sign, announcing in reasoning-shattering bold hues of red, white, and blue, 'Future Home of Bullock, Morgan and Richter Investment Holdings."

Kumar's nostrils flared with rage, Arjun's with terror. Smelling the anger, fear, and less ephemeral odors was a tall, muscular man spoke with a deep baritone voice designed to command rather than ask, even if used at a low volume.

"Smelling awfully rank there, 'Comrade' Patel," he noted, sticking his nose into Kumar's duster, then at the blood and sweat-stained shirt under it.

"Working hard will do that," Kumar replied, sizing the man up from head to toe, not ignoring the new Colt Revolver and blood-stained night stick in between. "New uniform, Sheriff Johnston?" Kumar shot back, fearing falling into his old cowardly habit of 'conflict avoidance' more than any bullet released from Morgan's chief law enforcer's gun.

"Colonel Johnston," Oliver Johnston replied, proudly pointing to the insignia on his US Army uniform. "Hired to keep Colorado for hard-working, God fearing, authority-respecting Coloradans. Unlike them…"

Johnston pointed Kumar's attention to a paddy wagon containing broken, starving men, women, and children. Chains were all of them, Army personnel of various ranks getting ready to escort them out of town.

"It's only natural," the middle-aged, Blue River-born and bred protector of the law, he so colorfully and somehow legally broke himself for at least the last decade, provided by way of explanation. "We gotta take care of our own, ya know."

"At the expense of everyone else, we SHOULD know?" Kumar respectfully replied. "Including, maybe…" He sniffed Johnston's jacket, tunic then shirt. "Whoever manufactured that new aftershave lotion. Makes you smell very 'sensitive' to your citizens' needs," he went on with a mocking lisp. "Except of course for the sensitive Two

Spirited and less than totally manly Indians, Negroes and Palefaces, you tarred, feathered and ran out of town," Kumar blasted into Johnston's enraged face with the super weapon of informed, calm and carefully assessed reason. After which he sought a second opinion, which was seldom wrong, if you listened to it right. "What do you think about that and everything else here, Arjun?" he asked his horse.

Arjun smelled Johnston, then winced in the most extreme expression of displeasure. Johnston pulled out his blood-stained, discreetly spiked billet, preparing to teach the equine beast a lesson in manners. With some prodding from Kumar, but mostly his own intent, the gelding turned around and laid a wad of soft brown reply from his anal orifice onto Johnston's new boots.

"Fertilizer, Sheriff Johnston," Kumar related, by way of orderly explanation. "All you need is a little water, and the crops will come up," the East Indian cowboy-philosopher mused at the demon possessing the Soul of a man who really wanted to do the right thing, according to theory and tall tales about the bad old days when Johnston protected Blue River from outlaws far worse than himself, or Morgan et al.

"I'll piss on your gravestone, you Commie Pagan Hindu alien bastard!" Sheriff and now Colonel Johnston barked out as he wiped the manure off his freshly polished Army boots. Johnston's attempt to remove the manure succeeded in pushing it deeper into the crevices of his footwear.

"First, Colonel, maybe one day, Comrade, Johnston," Kumar replied as he patted Arjun for administering karmic justice, and dharmic education, giving the horse his head as he headed back home up to the hills.. "I'm a Sikh, who prefers cowboy hats and buffalo knives to turbans and daggers, not a Hindu," the shoulder-haired, length and short-bearded East Indian Wild Westerner added. "Second, I'm a Democratic Socialist. Not a Fascist Communist, which is a contradiction in terms. Who believes that everyone can and should give according to their ability and take according to their needs.

And third…I was born in this country. Which I hope doesn't go the way of this one."

Kumar pulled out a book from the inner lining of his duster. "The Rise and Fall of the Roman Empire," he declared to Johnston, giving the voluntarily anti-intellectual officer a look at it. "I just started reading the second part, the 'fall.'"

"Which will never happen here!" Johnston yelled out with a clenched fist.

"Right, because men here wear pants and not togas or skirts," Kumar shot back.

"Because the rich will take care of the poor," the America First, second, and last Sheriff, now Colonel, declared. "Trickle down reality of economics."

"If you say so," Kumar conceded, after which he looked up at the sky, halting his horse. "What do you say about it?"

"Your Sikh Hindu Communist Pagan god?" Johnston volleyed back with a condescending smirk.

"No," the Cowboy, whose need to understand and change the way the world really worked exceeded the urge of any of his mounted friends, colleagues, and rivals to do so, replied. "That bird is my heavenly advisor, today anyway," he continued as he pointed to a hawk swooping down from the sky. On its own, or perhaps by means of some magical ability Kumar had to create reality from his head, the avian observer who seemed to have followed him from the high country down to the valley perched itself onto a tree limb above Johnston. Then the 'avian messenger' dropped its own urinary and fecal excrements on Johnson's head.

Johnston pulled out his Colt and shot at the bird. Thankfully, this time anyway, the Sheriff's usually sharp sense of vision was clouded by residual excrements on his eyes, allowing the avian participant in Kumar's drama, or perhaps Arjun's, to fly back up the thermals and head back to the mountains. Ironically, in the direction where Kumar was headed.

Drawn by something the bird was trying to tell him, along with the two-legged land walking creatures in town, Kumar opened the book about the Rise and Fall of the Roman Empire and proceeded on his way back home. "So, where were we?" he asked Arjun as he began reading. "In this book, that would be more effective if it had more jokes in it than hard facts, as we go back home to where WE belong."

CHAPTER 3

Books read by Spirit seeking humans said that just as there is an Avatar such as Jesus, Buddha, Krishna, and Mohamed for the human species, there are special advanced souls within each species for that species that look after its own kind. Arjun summoned the spirit of the equine Avatar to tell him why he had to endure yet another read from his 'master' Kumar from a book definitely not written by a humanoid Avatar. But, Arjun had spent much time training Kumar to be a kind, reliable, and intelligent caretaker who fed him more regularly than he ate himself. And Kumar had the good sense to maneuver Arjun with his legs, eyes, and voice rather than a harsh pull of the reins like his former owners did. Perhaps this time, the topic of the book being read or the reader would be somewhat interesting.

"Around 300 AD, the architectural wonders of Rome included the new, improved aqueduct system," Kumar, his eyes buried in the book, read aloud, with virtually no attention to what he was doing with the reins or his feet. Arjun smelled his way back to the trail leading to the shack in the hills, which now both rider and horse called home at an effortless, short-strided trot requiring only the brains in his feet to negotiate the way. Arjun found himself envisioning being somewhere else, as did Kumar, while the read went on. "An improved aqueduct system that brought in fresh water from the faraway Northern mountains to the elite urban citizenry in Rome who--- "

Awakened by a sign painted with non-naturally occurring colors made even more demonic by the sun reflecting on the metal behind it, Arjun opened his half-closed eyes. It was attached to a new, circular, 20-foot-high barbed wire fence in front of him. The newly constructed barrier closed off the previously accessible open range above it, which still, for now anyway, smelled of birch bark and wild alfalfa. Arjun stopped, abruptly awakening Kumar from visions of the past to the all too real present. 'Property of Morgan Richter and Associates Ranch?' Kumar read on the sign with shock, horror, and anger. He dismounted, pulled a rusted pair of pliers from his back pocket, and defiantly cut open the wired fence, being sure that it was wide enough for his legs to pass through and that his own writing he put on it was very legible. Arjun wasn't sure what the letters meant, but the suggestion, nay order, that the new owners copulate with themselves was certainly not complimentary.

"Western cowboys took the land away from the Indians last century," Kumar said as he rode Arjun up to a well-deserved snack of late fall alfalfa grass. "Karma says that Eastern bankers are the new assholes that are somehow required to keep the universe going in this century," Arjun's most recent human ward explained in words, not realizing that the meaning was already understood. "But as for what happened in the fourth century, according to the humorless, accurate, more than Alive big A writer," Kumar continued as horse and rider moved up the mountain to greener and, because of the lack of mining, farming, oil drilling, and coal excavation, taller grass.

Cows grazed around a pond that smelled…fishy, but from a different kind of fish than usual. The rocks seemed to be split open, sparking with green, gold, and yellow specks that Arjun didn't recognize. Unusual for this ride back home through a different route than normal. But there was one thing that was all too usual before the next read from this next book.

Kumar halted Arjun two seconds after the steed had already made that decision. He let the horse graze on the grass. The brown skinned Indian scholar-activist-cowboy reached into the recesses of his breast pocket and retrieved a cigar, which was thinner than a normal stogie but was thicker and rounder than a cigarette. As to what was within the paper, it was an all too familiar smell. Arjun shook his head, stomped his feet, back his ears back, and snortled.

"Hey, I let you eat grass, don't pull an attitude on me if I smoke it," Kumar protested as he took a toke from the reefer.

Arjun was endowed with a keen sense of smell, legs that could traverse 100 miles a day, hoofs that could grab hold of most surfaces, and the capacity to sleep standing up. But he did not have an opposable thumb that could rip the joint of locoweed from Kumar's mouth before it robbed his initiative, sense of reason, and ability to see the world as it

IS so he could effectively convert it to what it should be. But, being ridden by a stoned East Indian Truth seeker was better than having your mouth being ripped open by the hard pull of reins held by a drunken Colorado or Californian cowboy.

"Alright, back to reading," Kumar continued as the mobile reading room moved up the hill. "With colorful commentary that this tight assed and probably never got laid before his third year of marriage historical author wrote...." As quickly as a cutting horse could short-circuit a cow from going in the wrong direction, Kumar slipped into an accent mocking the English pseudo-monarchs who came to the wilds of Colorado to become big fish in small, manicured ponds. "...In the colonies of Inja' wrote down in black and white print that COMMANDS you to accept it is----"

Arjun halted, turning his ears and head to the right, suggesting to a stoned and self-absorbed Kumar a safer and perhaps even faster way to go home.

"Yeah....Fine...Your turn to pick the way home," Kumar conceded, thankfully. "But my turn to.." he continued, after which he took another toke from the locoweed containing mini cigar. He blew its smoke over Arjun's head, the wind sending it into the horse's nostrils. Kumar then prodded Arjun forward in the direction the steed knew was a route not occupied by bears, wolves, or, worse, toxic fumes of what some called 'black gold'.

"Wealth inequality in Ancient Rome was not any more than in any other civilization of its time. It maintained power for its elite, and comfort for their spouses and security for their associates," Kumar read as a scholarly English archeologist prick who never left the library. He then slipped into various dictions Arjun didn't recognize as a writer who got lost in the fog of a stoned stupor. "But the Greek language, theology, and architecture found their way into Roman society even when Rome had conquered Greece militarily. Yet again, the most powerful changes in Rome came not from the top, but from those closer to the bottom or on the bottom who…."

But what alarmed Arjun was not the rider about to fall off his back, but the country they were riding into. A plethora of rocks that had been split open by the most unnatural of causes dominated the landscape. Their inner skeletons were covered with strange pebbles within them. And there was the sight of dead cattle skulls in the distance. The odor of decaying flesh blew into Arjun's face now from his right, left, and ahead. All of the above were ignored by Kumar. Horse and rider were committed to moving forward with the story. The rider, anyway. One who has now lost or forfeited the ability to pronounce 'r's, replacing them with another consonant.

"The…weality of Ancient Wome and what brought down the Empire wasn't," Kumar continued. He pulled back the reins on Arjun, as he announced that there were 'wabbits' on the cliffs blown up by dynamite, or a thunder that was far more powerful than anything Arjun had experienced. Then Kumar sensed something else. "There are too many hunters here. Twying to kill the Yellow Wabbit? In a place that looks like…somewhere I was before. when I was hunting wabbits. Or maybe.."

Something moved in the bush. By smell, then sight, Arjun confirmed that it is a cow that was very wobbly. Something in its eyes and the way it attempted to move scared Arjun, and then Kumar.

"I wemember now! When the wabbits were hunting you and…me, and…" Before Kumar could reveal the details about THIS last lifetime memory, or how he felt about it, the wise, insightful, overly literate orator fell off the saddle, rolled several times over a grass covered wall of cow manure, then fell into a fetal position. He closed his eyes, then the book about the Fall of the Roman Empire. The rest of the story occurred behind Kumar's half closed glassy eyes. "But one could and will speculate that the real genius and significance of the larger and, for its time, high-tech aqueducts of the fourth century

in Ancient Rome was," Kumar said as his last words to the world of the conscious before fading into dreamland, or perhaps a nightmare. But it is someplace of potential importance to the 'real' world, somehow, Arjun suspected.

CHAPTER 4

Like the Yaqui Indians, Sigmund Freud, and dogs who always catch the 'wabbit' when chasing them while in deep slumber, Kumar felt that his dreams were more real than his experience in the 'awake' world. Or, at the very least, they were more instructive. This one seemed more real and instructive than any of the others.

Kumar awoke in this Vision as a Greek slave, Kumaris. He was clad in rags and in chains, standing in front of a table in a 'modest' villa worth several gazillion dollars, drachmas, or lira. Kumaris was being interviewed by a Roman Noble. One whose face was none other than Emerson Morgan, but even fatter and more laden down with shiny jewelry than his contemporary 'real world' presentation. Senator Morganius' presentation was topped off with an even more plastered-down comb-over on his balding head. Sheriff-Colonel Johnston stood next to 'Kumaris.' In this realm, he was a centurion, the homophobic 'man's man' wearing a toga which was more like a skirt than a kilt.

"So Kumaris," 'previous lifetime' Johnstonious grunted at Kumar with an upturned chin, his oversized and over-

tattooed arms folded. "Our generals who established order
        yet again in your region of Greece tell us that you
have special talents."

"Which we want, and therefore need," Morganius added
in an 'offer you are not allowed to refuse' confident tone.

"Like making you wear trousers instead of skirts? So
that you can show off your balls instead of your legs?"
Kumar replied as a counteroffer.

Johnstononius growled, grabbed Kumar by the throat,
and edged the blade of his sword onto his neck.

"No, Centurian Johnstonius," Morganius interjected.
"Remember who you work for…

"The people," Kumaris reminded his potential
executioner. "Who needs to buy your wares, promises, and
bovine detritus?"

"Bovine what, slave!?" Johnstonius roared out of his
mouth like a lion, trained, of course, to do so by trainer
Kumar at the moment.

"'Bullshit', for NOW Centurian Johnstonius," Senator
Morganius reminded his most non-thinking, and therefore
most useful, bodyguard. The fat Roman nobleman dismissed
the over-muscular Centurian with as minimal back-flip of his
hand as possible.

"Senator Morganious," Johnstonius informed his boss,
patron, and provider of structure, the 'free and independent'

Centurian needed more than he realized. "We shouldn't trust this…this…this…". Johnstonius' anger at Kumar was exceeded only by his embarrassment at a burst of wind coming in from the window that blew up his toga, exposing legs he had shaved recently, in private, of course. "This..this…"

"…Person of two spirits, or three, or four…or…five," the, to some anyway, pathologically excessive self-observing and people watching Greek slave offered regarding Johnstonius. "Not that there is anything wrong with that for me or any of you who…" he continued, after which he winked alluringly at Johnstonius.

Johnstonius lunged at Kumarus, trapping Morganius in between them.

"Enough!" Morganius commanded as the Senator tried to pull the Centurian off the non-repentant and perhaps courageous (rather than self-destructive) Greek slave. But as Morganius was far more skilled at hiring muscle than using it, he was tossed away by Johnstonius, landing on his ass near the wall. Coming to Kumarus's aid were none other than others of his new caste. Slaves from different regions of the Empire, namely Sam Longmorius, Buddy Emersonian, and Jake Halsinia, leaped in. Such prevented Kumarus's throat from being cut open by Johnstonius' dagger.

Stopping the Centurian from bashing the blade tip into Kumarus's right and left eye was none other than Leona Thunderstein from Germania, who kicked Johnstonius in his presumably oversized but most certainly sensitive balls.

While doing so, Leona lifted the key to the shackles o Kumar's wrist and legs from the Centurian's belt and unlocked them. Kumar gave Leona a nod of thanks. In response, she raised her eyebrows, saying, in Greek, sarcastically, 'now let's see you do something productive with your freedom, you moronic, head in the clouds whimp.'

"Slaves! Back to your duties!" Morganius commanded, his fat head finally reconnecting to the senses on his overweight body.

Sam, Jake, Bud, and Leona got back to menial tasks, breaking their backs but somehow not allowing their masters to break their spirits…for now. Approaching the table next was Senator Richterius and his Roman noble wife, Melissa Bullockia. Morganius bowed his head to his guests, and they bowed back, of course. By the way they sized each other up regarding what they were wearing and how they were wearing it, Richterius and Morgan were competitors out for themselves as well as colleagues pledged to serve the Roman people. The two noblemen complimented each other on their recent accomplishments, thanking the other for assisting in making those accomplishments possible. While they competed with each other as to who could make the most colorful dig at those under them both economically and politically to impress Melissa.

But Melissa had eyes for Kumarus. She motioned, behind her husband's back, that she wanted to have sex with the outspoken Greek slave, and would not accept no for an answer. Kumares was forced, by circumstance and curiosity to focus his visual attention on Melissa, who 'coincidently' worked her way between his eyeline and Leona's angry, and caring, eyes.

"My wife and I are planning a party for my fellow esteemed Senator Morganius, who owns and takes care of nearly 2,000 Romans of various stations and ranks," Richterius informed Kumarus, interrupting Melissa's proposal for…whatever.

"Over two thousand, one of whom used to be Dominus Richter's here," Morganius added. Kumarus was trying to figure out why these two men of power and influence wanted to impress rather than oppress him.

"Who," Richterius volleyed back with arrogance and pride regarding himself, "has obtained properties which now exceed those of my former Mentor and friend, Morganius, who…"

"…Is one of the most powerful citizens in Rome thanks, in part, to you, Ricterius who---" Morganius, stated.

"---knows that it is more important to please the people than to serve them," Ricterius replied.

"And to serve and please us…" Morganius added

"And the vast properties in my holdings…" Ricterius noted.

"And the people who make those holdings valuable…" Morganius pointed out, moving in for the kill.

"You need to do something about this, Senator Morganius," the younger ex-student shot at and into his old former teacher with that 'it's time to put you out to pasture, on MY farm, where you can be comfortable' look in his eyes.

Richterius plunked a jug of water in front of Kumarus, motioning for him to drink it. Such interrupted another round of flirting that Melissa had tried to start. It looked like murky shit, and tasted ever worse.

"Water from our rivers and the wells delivered by inferior stone aqueducts," Morganius explained. "Which---"

"---Are loaded with different kinds of detritus," Leona interjected as a fellow scholar.

"Crap, shit and 'poops' and other no good stuff," she continued, her head bowed as a illiterate slave.

"Which we can't serve to our guests," Richterius informed Kumarus, with a sense of urgency and fear.

"Or ourselves," Morganius asserted.

"Or our deservedly privileged and beloved children," Melissa added.

"But on top of the mountains, in the Alps, there is fresh, ultra clean water," Morganius said.

"So far," Leona added

Leona's Germania rage invoked the wrath of Roman-born, bred, and conditioned for obedience Johnston, who swung his bear-like arm towards her insolent face. But she ducked, causing him to fall head first into a vat of vomit which the Nobility filled at least three times a day after over-eating, over-drinking, and under-working.

"And if you can bring the magical pure, clean, and delicious water from the mountains, the FAR mountains," Richterius proposed to Kumar. "Down to us…"

"…And only us," Morganius added, thinking, or rather calculating, with the same Soul-disconnected mind.

"The elite and therefore Enlightened class…," Richterius added.

"We, and I, will be eternally grateful," Melissa added. She pursed her lips at Kumarus, then lowered the neckline on her dress, allowing Kumarus, and ONLY Kumarus a view of what was underneath it.

"And given your skill in designing, and building, delivery systems," Morganius added with a bow, and admiring those below from above, a smile. "We will grant your freedom."

"And anything you want," Richterius promised.

"And anyONE you want," Melissa added, placing herself, 'coincidently' between Leona and Kumarus, hindering the view of the former by the latter.

"To make this delivery system, you will need the right materials," Leona added, from the side of her mouth while cleaning up even more debris on the floor that Melissa had now intentionally thrown her way to clean up. "Given your knowledge of metallurgy, architecture, and medicine to deliver specific material. To specific people…for the good of all people." Leona looked up at Kumarus, continuing the rest of her suggestions to him in his native dialect of Greek. "Lead!!!! That fucks up the brain, and the body. To be delivered to them," she sneered regarding the Romans. "And only them."

"What did she say?" Centurian, and soon to be Private or Servant, Johnstonius barked out from his assigned position guarding the door.

"Nothing important," Kumarus said to Johnstonius with respect for the human he could be if he had to courage to stop being the man he thought he had to be. He treated himself to a quick 'gotta have a future with her anyway I have to' glance at Leona. Then to Morganius, Richterius, and finally, Melissa. "Nothing important to you important people anyway. Just that…Hippocrates said I was his favorite pupil. The brightest, smartest, and cleverest, who deserves and HAS to be paid big Drachmas by his patients."

"A lot of words there that you translated from what this Germanic bitch said," Johnstonius barked out regarding Leona's untranslated suggestion.

"This dialect of Greek is a very condensed language," Kumarus explained, after which he looked at Leona, hoping that she was impressed with his ability to lie creatively and effectively, which she was. "Yes, a very condensed language, my dialect of Greek and hers."

"Which you will teach us?" Morganius requested rather than commanded, as was the manner of semi-literate powerful Romans who wanted to advance themselves as more cultured and fashionable Nobles.

"While these slaves built the super aqueduct that you designed," still Centurian Johnstonius sneered, no doubt envisioning the hard labor breaking the men's backs and demolishing Leona's spirit.

"Which will make us, including perhaps you, more popular, liked, and respected, by the people that matter anyway, " Morganius offered.

"But in the meantime, Doctor Kumarus," Melissa interjected just as Kumarus allowed a plan to materialize in his now swelled head. She took him by the arm, like a Noble Woman escorted by a Noble Man, taking him into a more private area of the multi-purpose orgy room. "People   tell me that I am as lovely as Pandora, but I'd like to be as beautiful as Athena…With your medical skills and connections, can you adjust these?" she continued, pointing to her breasts and face.

"No problem," Kumarus replied in Hindi, causing suspicions with the Roman elite, as well as with the slaves who he would perhaps liberate when executing the plan to screw up the minds, finances and decision making processes of their current masters. "I mean," he said in a tongue they all could understand. The specifics as to what Kumarus meant, and who would be told what, were abruptly revealed.

CHAPTER 5

"And according to the theory of most scholars, it was not sword of the Hun or the bravery of the oppressed classes that brought down the rich and powerful of Rome," Leona read from Kumar's book under the light of a full moon while the brown skinned EAST Indian lay on his back, slobber coming out of the left side of his mouth, snoring from his oversized nostrils. "And according to what is not in most historical records, there indeed was a distribution of wealth to less fortunate Souls, as there indeed was something in the super aqueducts which leaked into the water drunk by mostly the rich and powerful, which was..."

"Lead," Leona heard from what seemed like an echo from the past. It was something that happened to her a lot lately, particularly when the moon was full. "Which is...maybe here?" Kumar continued as his eyes opened up, and then the rest of his senses decided to work together rather than separately. "Like what happened to them!" he said, pointing to white lights in the bush. Closer examination by Leona revealed that it was a reflection of the moonlight upon dead cattle skulls. "Lead did them in!" Kumar insisted.

"Or, something else," Leona suggested with her much-ignored by both White and Red men, advanced faculty of reason. Knowing that such a required proof, Leona retrieved a permanently borrowed Geiger counter from the saddle bag of her horse. She then put the smelling end of it on the pond and the fluorescent marbles within the cracked open rocks around it. The ticking spooked Kumar out of whatever century he had visited in dreams to the present.

"What the fuck it that?" Kumar blurted out of a dropped jaw, his ass having landed in yet another pile of cow droppings.

"A toy I stole from the chemistry lab where the kindly, God fearing and very professorial instructor said he was hungry for some 'red meat' after class," Leona explained. She perused the area with the Spiritually primed third eye she inherited from her Shaman Grandfather, while triangulating the source of the radiation with the geometrical precision and mathematical prowess her Grandmother brought to every activity of Native life before most of those activities were officially outlawed. "A Paleface professor who said after praising me for being the smartest and wisest student in the class after the 'tell me only what I have to know for the exam' rich, white students had left the lab,.....that he was 'hungry for some red meat'"

"Maybe he really wanted a steak," Kumar offered with the calm, stabilizing voice of his, which made everyone else more 'harmonic' with the universe. But, as always, it drove a wedge of disruptive fire into Leona's spine. It went all the way up to her constantly fast thinking 'galloping to the next thoughts' brain, which she refused to bring down to a trot, or even a lope. "Professors can get hungry for a steak, with fries. And to share a meal and only a meal with students who WANT to learn. It makes them feel purposeful, appreciated, and.---"

"----This Geiger counter detects uranium," Leona explained regarding the Geiger counter.

"Uranium being a Lakota god?" Kumar asked.

"No, you idiot!" she barked back at the scholar who was an expert in most everything except hard, real-life science.

"A Lakota goddess?" he inquired, sincerely. Great Spirit bless and help him.

"Uranium, Atomic number 92," Leona reiterated. "Something in THIS universe, not the one you visit when you," she continued, having smelled the stash of 'wacko tobacco' in his breast pocket. She grabbed hold of the weed, threw it into the dirt, and buried it before Kumar, with his slowed-down reflexes, could retrieve it.

"Hey, you people burn sweetgrass," he protested, while trying to sift leaves and seeds from the overwhelming dirt around them.

"Which, unlike that 'soul opening grass of YOURS, makes our reflexes faster and our minds sharper and our spirits more hardworking."

"I have a right to like, ya know, relax, Leona. Take some time off from the Workers Revolution.".

"Which doesn't include Redskinned Revolutionaries!" Leona pointed out.

"Your choice, not ours," Kumar replied, shooting back the accusational arrow directly into a bull's-eye inside of Leona.. "In a world where----"

Leona looked up at the sky, feeling the future calling her to see at least some of it so that the present could be moved forward into it, kicking, screaming, and, yes, dancing. "A really hard rain HAS to fall, and should," she asserted, hoped, and prayed while Kumar looked at the cows coming out of the bush, congregating around them both. "You White, Yellow, Black and even Brown skinned Palefaces created the Dust Bowl by making the land bleed by putting the plow to it. It destroyed the natural grasslands and replaced them with crops that blow away with the wind. When it will end, the answer is blowing in the wind. And as I continue to say things that I wrote, which someone will probably culturally appropriated by someone else who—"

"---These cows are not doing so good," Kumar interjected, this time bringing Leona out of her dream world into the present. Indeed, some of the bovine, perhaps reincarnated human, souls seemed depressed. Some stared into space. Some walked in circles, some looked at the same tree, rock, or fallen branch again and again, as if they had forgotten what their eyes had seen ten seconds ago. Some merely walked around with a wobbly gate. One of the bovines, who seemed to be more lost within its own skin and home range than the others, by intention or accident, walked at a brisk pace towards a cliff that would put anything that ventured onto it into a permanent fall.

"No!!!" Kumar yelled at the cow. He rushed over to it, diverting it with a stick, screams, and finally his fist to remain on the stable side of the cliff belonging to the still living. In the process of doing so, he saw, then brought to Leona's attention to bovine bones and corpses below the hill. They were also the skeletons of half-eaten cattle. Bushes and small trees with berries on them were interspersed between them. The carrion dining on the cattle seemed stoned, those who were still alive anyway.

"There's something really strange that's going on with these guys," Kumar noted, yet again.

"And gals?" Leona inquired.

"Mostly the guys," replied the cowboy who knew as much, or more, about domestic cattle as Leona's ancestors knew about wild bison. "In a herd that I used to know…before someone blasted a hole into these rocks. Looking for oil, copper, gold, dead human bodies, or… well, fuck if I know. The bulls and young ones who still could be bulls who are still alive are depressed. Some have fucked up memory. None of them want to extend out of their territory, or extend out their dick. They're useless. Suicidal. I don't give a shit if I live or die zombies who have 'fuck me over if you want or need to' signs on their foreheads. A state of no mind that I am painfully familiar with."

"And the girl cattle?" Leona asked, as both a feminist and a scientist.

"A little wobbly," Professor Patel noted, pointing Leona's attention to three female bovines getting from point A to B with far more determination than grace. "But they get to where they want to go, and still have the will to know where they want to go and need to go."

"And situations below the neck with these creatures, I mean, perhaps reincarnated souls?" Leona asked, thinking that, perhaps, Kumar's theories about past lives could give her answers regarding what was happening in these hills that her people had used but never owned as hunting, grazing, and berry gathering grounds. And we're still using it as such.

Kumar jumped down from one of the dead cattle, then offered his hand to Leona to join him. Due to her admittedly poor ability to stay erect on steep ground, she accepted. He picked up kidneys from the half-eaten belly of a, thankfully dead, bovine before a crow could eat it.

"No!" Kumar blasted at the black avian diner. "'Hercules' here died of kidney failure," he said regarding the once-alive and, according to the size of his family jewels, virile bull.

"After thinking that he himself was a failure," Leona proposed.

The crow attempted to eat berries off a half-stripped bush. Kumar shoo'd him away. He asked Leona to give him the sensitive end of the Geiger counter. The lights on the strange box he had never seen, which had only recently been devised, lit up like fireworks on the Fourth of July. The clicks on it were louder than a swamp filled with crickets announcing their presence on a 100-degree, humid night. Bird skeletons lay under the berry bush.

"And if we can make American success stories think they are failures, like Hercules did," Kumar suggested, after which he scratched his clean-shaven chin like so many professors did with their bearded ones.

"This smells like dangerous medicine, Kumar," Leona said, sharing a third brain with her fellow brown-skinned expatriate who didn't quite fit in with his people, just like she, truth be told, didn't integrate well with hers.

Kumar moved to another bush and tested the berries there. Less ticking was on it. His life-seeking eyes picked up something inside of it. He reached in and retrieved a nest of birds deep within the branches. He moved them gently to another bush, whose berries did not light up the machine.

"And letting the fuck heads on top keep fucking our people and yours is a safe and necessary thing to do," Kumar gave voice to, after which he pontificated a proverb in what, if you used a lot of imagination, sounded like Lakota.

Leona allowed herself a well-deserved laugh.

"Hey...I was trying to be profound here!" Kumar protested.

"And maybe more revealing than you want to be," Leona replied, self-observing the edge of her lips move upwards.

"So, what did I say?" Kumar asked.

"I wish I could have a chocolate flavored vagina, loosely translated," Leona replied.

Kumar pulled out a dictionary from his back pocket. "What I meant to say is…" he said while searching the weather-beaten pages.

Leona laid her hand on his arm lovingly. "Tell me what's in your naïve heart, hard head, and

up your fart emitting ass. In English…please."

CHAPTER 6

When Emerson Morgan woke up in the morning, it felt like just another day in Blue River, Colorado, a town he decided would be transformed into another Boston. But according to Morgan's agenda, it would be even richer and more prestigious than the city he grew up in, and would not go back to. Not until he had shown his Blue Blood family back East that he was a far more accomplished Colonial Master than any of them were.

If he succeeded in this Western town, he broke down so that he could build it back up into his and American Capitalism's image, perhaps he would wake up rested rather than exhausted by nightmares about being sent back to Harvard Business School or Beacon Hill Prep. It was there that, as a middle-aged man, he failed every course he had aced on his own or cheated his way to such as a younger man.

Morgan diplomatically asserted in the back-to-back meetings at his opulent office with investors and debtors, he was the undisputed King of this town, the county, and, according to all projections, most of the state. He claimed that every day he was having more of an influence on the commoners who served him, and therefore ultimately themselves, than he had planned. Most particularly when the Kumar Patel, Sikh cowboy who usually smelled like East Indian food, high country sweat, or tobacco that reeked of Pagan incense, and whose clothing was more like the rags Socrates wore when day dreaming in Ancient Athens than what established gentlemen at established universities donned, appeared before him. Kumar had taken a bath in a tub rather than the river, in a real suit. His face was smoothly shaved rather than colorfully stubbled. Seated next to him in another chair which, by design of course, made even a six foot five man's face lower than five foot five Morgan's, was 20th century Anarchist Redskin Leona. She was clad in a generously fringed and colorfully beaded outfit that was as authentic to her ancestral culture as it was alluring to a man of any culture.

What the 'finally giving into the system' cowboy and his 'taking her place as an alluring squaw rather than aspiring to be chief' Injun girl friend wanted, was a source of curiosity to Morgan. Still, there are other matters to be dealt with, requiring Morgan to take the gold watch his grandfather had passed down to him. "You said you have an idea that would make this county, state, and country a Paradise," the overfed tycoon said to the underfed commoners. "You have sixty seconds, as time is money. Go!" he continued, noting the minute hand on the watch, leaning back on the cushioned chair he converted into a throne.

Kumar pulled a jar of berries from the briefcase bearing initials that were not his own. He offered Morgan both a smell and a taste. "Special berries from a special place," he said with a slow, confident voice, and a bit of upscale Bostonian English to his diction.

"Place of big medicine," Leona added, with an accent that sounded very 'Injun.' Of course, she dropped the articles and verbs. "My grandmother's medicine. Now my place and my medicine."

"Now hers. And we propose, now yours," Kumar added, interrupting Morgan's ocular upwardly moving survey of Leona's exposed legs, shapely hips, and perfectly sized breasts.

"Special healing powers for body and mind," 'Injun goddess' Leona said, with the kind of promise worthy of the alluring Oracles of Delphi in Ancient Greek.

"That makes 'sweetgrass smoking' brown skinned cowboy waste forty seconds," Morgan said, recalling that these Oracles offered Truth seekers mind-altering mushrooms prior to answering their questions. He turned to Leona. "And makes you, the only member of your tribe with enough brain, sand and, if you decided to use rather than hide it, sexual appeal to get a real education, talking without using articles like a----"

"---This shit works!" the traditionally clad Injun Einstein barked back like a defiant Union Organizer at the docks in Boston Harbor. "As proven in rats, hamsters, and mice," she continued as an accomplished, but still young, academic researcher. She yanked a pile of papers from Kumar's, plopping them onto Morgan's desk. "And---"

"---And three, two, one," Morgan interjected as he counted down the second hand on his watch.

"---And tested on me!" Leona shot back, after which she grabbed hold of the berries, throwing one of them down her throat.

Morgan was not convinced or impressed until she ate another berry, then another, then two more beyond that, each snack of the magic potion accompanied by an alluring sexual gesture. Morgan put down his watch, sat back, and with the most minimal of movements of his blister-free, manicured fingers, motioned for Leona to continue.

"I still have contacts at the University I went to. did some experiments there, and at home, which for certain financial and political reasons, remain unpublished," the traditionally dressed Lakota woman rattled off with an upright spine, elevated chin and sharply pronounced consonants more consistent with an upstart but upwardly moving Grad Student at a REAL university located, of course, EAST of the Mississippi. "With enough n values to come up with valid statistics. Using ANOVA testing of all groups, proving to a 98% certainly level that whatever is in these berries and the water that feeds them does indeed generate axonal growth and neuronal network expansion in male animals that makes them far superior to any of their competitors in the control groups."

Her rapidity of speech, making her sound even more intelligent, compelled Morgan to look at the data in front of him. "And the lower dose groups as well. The ability to intuit, memorize, deduce, and act assertively against all obstacles provided by nature or setbacks inflicted by one's…competitors," she continued.

Convinced by what appeared to be scientific logic and a businessman's intuition, Morgan reached into the jar of berries, eager for a taste. Leona slapped his hand in the manner of the many commoner Dominatrix escorts who he wished would become his wife. But he had many times declined the offer, as surrendering control to a woman was something a powerful man who wanted to stay powerful only did in private.

"No…Let me," Leona said, seeming to be the composite of every girl toy and mastress bitch Morgan had accessed on his way up to the top, both here in the to be conquered West, and back in the already over established East.

Leona dipped her slender, mangled fingers into the jar, then put a berry into Morgan's mouth. He smiled in delight, his tongue having tasted her intact flesh, a tinge of her blood on it.

"Great man about to become Superman, want more?" Leona asked.

Morgan nods his head 'yes', his stare fixed on her even more exposed breasts, as she places another berry onto his tongue.

"Then…Great Spirit says to listen to the proposition from Brown skinned Cowboy," Mistress Leona suggested and commanded.

Kumar seemed to feel confident. A man who pulled himself up from his previous station. Until Leona spat out, pointing to Kumar, "Listen to proposition from Sikh cowboy, whose horse is smarter than he is."

Kumar felt insulted. But he held back a well-hidden fist he made in anger.

"… but…after eating these berries," Leona continued to Morgan, regarding Kumar. "Cowboy dreamer, head in the clouds, Comrade Patel---"

"---had enough brains to dress like a respectable Free Market Capitalist real American man," Morgan surmised, and gave voice to.

"And he took a bath," Leona said as she sniffed a now poker-faced Kumar, whose chin was held up in compliant-with-the-system pride rather than rebellion. "In the waters around these berries."

"---That, yeah…gave me an idea that will not only make you richer now. And immortality remembered later," former Comrade now Citizen Patel said regarding Morgan.

"For being a brilliant humanitarian instead of a rich businessman. And an even greater American. Yes?" Leona added.

Kumar took out papers from his briefcase, respectfully placing the blueprints and cost projections in front of Morgan. "A gentleman's club for top-end gentlemen…And only them…A man's only place which…" Kumar turned to Leona. "Mister Morgan and I have to discuss the particulars here…Between men. Which of course you understand.".

"Sure…I understand," Leona replied with her head bowed, her eyes looking downward. After which, she snatched Morgan's golden stopwatch, pressing the timer. "You 'gentlemen' have five minutes," she proclaimed with just enough rebellion in her voice to sound interesting, but not dangerous to the status quo.

"And if we take six minutes?" Kumar asked her.

"There are other gentlemen who are eager for new opportunities to get richer now and get more famous in the future, in other towns that…well…," Leona related with as much confidence as Morgan had ever heard from any woman on her way up the ladder. Including his newest love in the bedroom and fellow conqueror in the board room, Melissa Bullock.

While Leona sauntered her way to the door, letting her ass do more talking than her succulent mouth did, Morgan imagined what it would be like to cajole Melissa out of business associate Richter's bedroom. And to get Leona into his own, experiencing them both at the same time. Or seeing them fight each other over who would be his favorite.

But, business before pleasure. "So," Morgan said, turning to Kumar. "Show me my, I mean, your idea."

"The location for this Gentleman of Gentlemen's club, Sir," Kumar said as he laid down the aerial map.

"Which we own now," Morgan noted. "Good," he checked in his head regarding the property he had already acquired, legally this time.

"And the design of the facilities, Sir," Kumar continued, presenting Morgan with the architectural plans.

"Sound," Morgan said after quickly assessing its essential features.

"And the people I propose to build and operate it," the converted to common sense Capitalism said, offering Morgan a list of citizens. "Who will keep this New Order and how it does what it does for the county, state, and country secret, Sir," Patel continued with an even deeper bow. It was the third time Kumar had said 'Sir' to ANYONE in Blue River, according to rumor anyway.

"And you swear this on…?" Morgan inquired, after leaning back on his throne, looking down at and into this new apprentice who, according to rumor anyway, valued his honor more than his life.

"I swear the delivery and confidentiality of all of this on the life of my horse, Arjun," Patel pledged.

"Which I will hold you to, you know," Morgan proclaimed with a raised index finger.

"Understood and appreciated," Kumar replied, with something Morgan had rarely seen in any of his subordinates, associates, or potential wives. Sincerity and commitment, the kind that could not be faked.

Leona waited impatiently in the waiting parlor outside of Morgan's office. She looked at her watch, noting that the time had passed well beyond the five minutes she had commanded and the six Kumar had requested. Finally, after three times that allocated time, Kumar emerged, smoking a cigar. A big one, which reeked of Fat Cat Paleface tobacco rather than his own brand of 'High Country Weed'. But this time his head was in the clouds with something more frightening to Leona than past lifetime memories of past glories he wanted to dwell in, or inflict upon the present.

What Kumar appeared to be on the outside was what he now seemed to be on the inside. A man of high station who was being introduced by Morgan and Richter to other men of high station, and low moral values. Who was being eyed as a new mark by Melissa Bullock as she passed by? All of the Paleface moguls ignored by Leona, of course.

Finally, after seeing Kumar indulge in small talk with words she couldn't hear but smelled of power, which could corrupt even the purest of souls, Leona noted 'Citizen Patel' stride her way with a gait that said proud, loud, and obnoxious. "You're late" she said to him in Lakota as she got up, as an obedient woman AND squaw. According to the script, she walked head bowed behind Kumar as he strolled toward the exit door of the Mansion.

"And you're...hmmm..." Kumar said from the side of his mouth to her.

"Necessary for this plan of OURS to happen," she said in Lakota.

"As am I," he asserted, in English, having completely understood her words and feelings regarding many things that had happened. And even more was to transpire.

As the two commoner Commie Comrades who had conned the richest Capitalist con man in Colorado exited the ornate Mansion, they heard, saw, and then smelled the desperation on dirty, gruesome-looking prisoners in a chain gang, heavily laboring to make the grounds beautiful. Kumar walked past them, pretending to be upscale. As the prisoners were supervised by highly armed soldiers under Johnston's command, Leona did her best to appear subservient. She hoped that the most recent prisoners to the chain gang, who had been inadvertently let in on the plan by Kumar, when he was stoned on his 'special brand' of sweetgrass, didn't wink or smile at her or him.

"So, you were able to pick up which berries had uranium in them and which ones didn't," Kumar asked Leona regarding the jar of berries she had eaten and the ones she allowed and required Morgan to sample.

"I think so. Hope so," she replied from the side of her mouth. Her head was bowed even lower when Johnston gazed at her legs, apparently not noting who they belonged to, thankfully. "Besides, the REAL rodent data we came up with, using the rodents I stole from the research lab and pet stores says that low doses of uranium do not affect female mentation, aspirations, or execution of plans to expand perspective and knowledge."

"Where did you learn to do all of that?" Kumar asked, intuiting yet another secret about the Lakota woman and Redskinned bombshell who had promised to never lie to him with 'forked tongue', or a 'fuck me now' smile.

"I became a research scientist without going to a research Science school. Merged art and science. Aspired to be the next Albert Einstein but without the weird hair and German accent," her reply, voiced assertively and with upturned chin, once she was sure that prisoners and guards had focused their attention on the building, yet another opulent stone wall around the mansion.

"No," Kumar replied. "I mean, I wanted to know…How you learned to lie like that."

"Same place we savages learned how to scalp our enemies."

"We Palefaces, I know… Which I'm not!"

"Half of you is."

"Not the half that's doing all of this!"

"And that, my naïve yet caring Revolutionary for the people, scares me." Leona offered as her final statement on matters past, and uncertain situations that had to be set into motion in the very soon-to-emerge future.

CHAPTER 7

Why the barn and adjoining cabin used by the Wild Bunch three decades ago as a hold up location was still standing was a mystery, the wind and soft ground under portions of it had converted it into a tilted structure which made the leaning tower of Pisa look like a solid dwelling that was exactly 90 degrees from solid ground. Perhaps it was because Sam Pickering, master carpenter and, because he didn't get caught, skillful outlaw who rode with the Wild Bunch, had done a good job constructing the facility. A far better job than any of the industrially rather than practically trained construction workers in town, he could have hired. Or perhaps Sam's ghost was still hanging around in the place, holding up a pillar and sneaking a nail or two into the posts to prevent the walls and roof from caving in. But three things were true about the location known to the locals in Blue River, and not yet the historians from Denver or Chicago.

Firstly, the dust and snow storms that had torn down so many structures in town were unable to turn The Hold Up into a pile of fragmented lumber and rusted nails. Second, there was more swamp and quicksand around the location than solid ground. In the past such had prevented many a lawman, creditor, or nagging wife looking for her absent husband the ability to reaching the clandestine location. And third, because of the two aforementioned problems, or legends, no realtor tried to buy The Hold Out, or the land around it.

Kumar found out about the only safe route to The Hold Out through, of all people, his boss, friend, mentor, and surrogate father, multi-seasoned cowboy Sam Longmore. When Longmore was a boy, the aging Pickering had entrusted him with his various stories about real outlaws. Because outlaws were not protected by the law, they had to be honest in order to survive and get anything of worth done before they were hung, or fade into obscurity. The stories were passed down to Kumar, and only Kumar, by Sam. In part, this was because Sam Pickering's story was not unlike Kumar's Sikh Grandfather herdsman who waged war in various ways in India against the oppression of the Colonial British Masters until he was hanged.

Kumar had thought long and hard about giving selected people the route to The Hold Up. But it felt both appropriate and necessary to discuss at that location a plan which required both unity and secrecy. They all came in dead of night under a half moon, some by car, some by horse, some on foot. All of them made it without losing a vehicle, steed, or even a boot. Kumar had brought the 'Worker's Rights Meeting Hall' official sign away from Morgan's burn pile in town. It was solidly and symmetrically placed above the unlocked, until all invited parties arrived anyway, the barn door. "For tonight" was hand-painted under it, of course.

As someone had to coordinate things, even in a cooperative experiment, Kumar stood in front of the congregation atop a platform. He sat behind a 'table' made by placing an old door over two logs that were, sort of, the same height. Leona stood behind him.

Doc Wilson opened up the discussion, getting straight to the point, as a Doctor who wasted no time in informing his patients about how they could extend their life as best as possible, or deal effectively with its impending end. He stood up on his exhausted feet, looking over the real data Leona had obtained by testing the effects of uranium on rodents she had stolen from the local college, as well as those she had trapped in the woods. The site of those studies was Kumar's cabin. Wilson scratched his head, a reservoir of where old ideas merged with new ones on their own terms, which was going balder with each year he agonized over the best way to cure the diseases rather than merely remedy the symptoms his patients brought to him. "So, this rodent data says that we can drug the confident rich into becoming the self-doubting poor, by taking away their pride, inflated egos, and confidence."

"Specifically, their short-term memory and competitive skills," Leona asserted as a calm, logical research scientist whose convictions never exceeded what the data proved. "Dulling the emotions that make them competitive, cruel, and vicious. And effectively evil!," she continued as a Passion possessed Warrior.

"Which potentially, can send them into the nuthouse," the critically-thinking ex-researcher who defiantly became a passionately driven clinician pointed out.

"Temporarily, in a few isolated cases, they may have to be treated in mental wards," Kumar interjected calmly. "Where they can be treated by humanistic physicians like you, Doc. But with the plan we have in mind, and on paper, we'll never send any of them to the coffin."

"But even if we do, we treat the disease of Capitalistic greed that's killing REAL Americans by cutting out the cancer, that wouldn't be so bad…." Union activist by necessary rather than choice, Dubois shouted out as he stood up. He clenched his good hand with a fist that had only three remaining fingers due to 'industrial accidents' inflicted by the bosses. He had scars on his face inflicted by undercover Pinkertons who were hired to teach him a lesson after talking Union talk to workers in the tavern after a 12-hour day. "Killing these rich bastards who are starving everyone else into the grave, with 'industrial accidents' is something that, well, if it happens, it happens."

"But not necessary," Kumar offered.

"Yet…We, I, anyway, fought a war in the trenches to stop rich and powerful tyrants from

taking over Europe, and this country," DuBois asserted. Such delivered an arrow that silenced Kumar, as he had never been tested in ANY combat involving fists or firearms on either side of the Atlantic, or Pacific.

"There will always be tyrants," Father Smith said as he stood up, humbly bowing while delivering the calm assertion. "Jesus said we have to educate and, yes, love them, and endure them," he offered to the congregation, including 'undecideds' Jake, Buddy, Sam, Elsa, and her mother, Mary.

"Which is why Jesus asked the moneylenders in the temples to leave, nicely, right Father?" Dubois countered. "Gotta fight fire with fire."

"Which can burn us also," Smith volleyed back with the assertion of mind, body, and spirit.

"Spoken as a coward," Dubois smirked accusingly with a battle-scarred face at Father Smith, whose body had not acquired a single blow from an armed or unarmed man. Knowing, as Kumar sensed, the proof of such, which, for the moment, would not be voiced.

"I'm concerned about what happens to us, spiritually," Smith offered from the bottom of his tortured, conflicted, and secret heart. "And if we do this, what are the chances of us getting sick or worse because of this uranium exposure?

"When we build the meeting center at the Uranium power spots, we'll be wearing protective suits," Leona replied, bringing the focus of attention to matters physical rather than metaphysical. Such reminded Kumar that he had to now do something in the real world rather than further expand into the realm of ideals and ideas. That beast his down to earth, and his 'downer' merchant father in Sacramento is called 'accountability'. "We wear protective lead suits, gloves, and masks." Leona pulled out the stolen

Geiger counter, boldly showing off the University label on it. "And routinely measure exposure with this," she continued, retrieving a Geiger counter from her backpack."

"And when we serve up old time country moonshine and traditional berry bannock

when Mister Morgan's friends and bosses come out here," Buddy asked, more scared of the unseeable beast of radiation than he ever was of very seeable and hearable Leona. "Ta this Secret Society city slicker dude ranch we're gonna build? The grass, berries, and water out here can irradiate all of us."

"Who eats what and when, and who bathes in what, that's up to Leona," Kumar assured Buddy. "And, as we all know, or should know about Leona, she---"

"----Can convince any man to do or be anything she wants," Sam interjected, reading Kumar's mind, while trying to drive a very private lesson into the East Indian cowboy's Soul with his eyes. "So I've heard."

"And know," Jake added, looking accusingly at Kumar.

"Hey! I'm my own man!" Kumar asserted to every member of the audience he had summoned to The Hold Out. "Right?" he asked, looking at Leona.

"Of course," she assured him, and perhaps only him.

"And I don't need the approval of any woman or man or man who is less of a man than others to approve of me,"

Kumar boldly exclaimed, feeling his lying Pinochio nose growing bigger with each word. "Right?" he asked Sam and Leona.

"Sure," Sam said with words that allowed whoever needed to believe they were true to accept them as such.

"I suppose yer someone who don't need any woman to laugh at your

Jokes. Or man ta like your propositions," Jake challenged Kumar with, not unexpectedly.

"It's a proposal, Comrade Jake," Doc Wilson reminded the foul-mouthed and even less pleasing to look at orphan brat who was expected to live up to his father's legacy of being a cowboy's all-American cowboy, but never could, no matter how hard he tried.

"Hey Doc, watch who yer callin' Comrade, Doc!" Jake yelled back, more concerned with present ideologies than past inadequacies.

"We're in the new, hopefully not found out about, Workers' Union Hall. It's just an expression," Wilson reminded the hot-headed cow puncher whom he had treated for so many injuries, both accidental and unconsciously self-inflicted.

"An un-American expression! Ever heard of the Red Scare?!!!" Jake blasted back, rising to his feet, his hand clenched in a Union busting fist that would not let go until his knock out the nearest 'Comrade', or friend. "The Red s Scare, which is---"

"---What happens on your crotch when you get too drunk and think your horse is a woman who forgot to shave her legs that year," Kumar interjected as a joke, which did cajole Wilson and Jake into a chuckle, followed by Buddy, then Dubois. But the person Kumar was trying to impress with his humor, even more than himself, didn't laugh. Leona's face showed something worse than feminist indignation at the joke, which Mary, Edna's mother, displayed. No, Leona's sympathetic sigh without a condescending eye roll clearly indicated pity for Kumar's lack of wit and intellect.

"Hey, a Socialist joke to bring us all together," Kumar explained to Leona. He then turned to the others as if they were a single herd. He let his eye find the lead bull or cow so they would lead the rest to where he wanted and needed them to go, as a cohesive unit. "A socialist joke that lets us look at and into ourselves. So… two Socialists walk into a bar…"

"…While this Cowboy walks out of this morally and biologically

Dangerous Revolutionary experiment," Sam Longmore asserted calmly and compassionately as he stood up and made his way to the exit door. The old but certainly not defeated cowMAN then turned to Buddy and Jake, cowboys whom was determined and sworn to pass the rugged individualist Sagebrush torch. Buddy, we got cattle depending on us," he related as a surrogate father and friend.

"Those are now owned by someone else." The usually silent and compliant Buddy pointed out, while firmly keeping his saddle-worn down ass on the log which was his chair.

"A temporary situation, son," the nearly completely cattle-less veteran rancher assured Buddy. "This is America. Where hard, honest work is always rewarded."

"With harder times," Buddy reminded Sam, the gurgling in his underfed stomach solidifying the point.

Sam then turned to Jake. "Ya comin'?"

"Not yet," replied Jake, the only attendee whom Kumar didn't directly invite to the top-secret meeting. "I wanna see what happens with this reshuffling of the gets started. See where the money and power go," he continued, remaining in his seat. It left Kumar to ponder the same question, in deeper ways than he bargained for.

"Or who the money and power goes to, Jake?" Sam countered. "Like maybe it could be… you?"

"Or to any of us, Sam," Jake shot back to the only one in town who would still hire him, addressing him by his first name for the first time. "Which is better than any a' them who's on top of all of us now!"

Each member of the congregation nodded 'yes' to the assertion by the new Convert to the Cause. Starting with Dubois, then Wilson, then Buddy, then, after the thought had spread to everyone else, finally Father Smith.

"Right, Comrades," Smith said after deep reflection. He then looked up to the sky above the still present but now creaky roof. "Right, Father?" Kumar waited for a reply from the Unseen Boss, whom he, on good days anyway, was more of a well-meaning friend than a sadistic task master.

Meanwhile, the infection of doubt went through every 'Comrade' in the barn, including Leona. Until, finally, Father Smith's quivering lips broke into a wide smile, his bloodshot eye shining brighter than any star in the heavens. "Yes. Our Heavenly Father, and the Great Spirit, says yes!" Smith reported regarding his dialog with the Almighty. "Hallelujah!" he declared with an unbridled joy neither Kumar nor anyone else had seen the worrywart display. With that, Smith began singing the Internationale, with the zeal of a Baptist Revivalist, and, to everyone's amazement, a voice that provided the lyrics with musically inspiring notes that didn't waver. "Arise, ye prisoners of starvation! Arise, ye wretched of the earth! For justice thunders condemnation. A better world's in birth!"

"No more tradition's chains shall bind us. Arise, ye slaves, no more in thrall!" came from a handful of other voices. "The earth shall rise on new foundations. We have been naught, we shall be all!" Kumar self-observed himself singing, badly, but accurately with regard to the lyrics.

"'Tis the final conflict," Leona added, with an almost operatic voice, in English rather than her own Native tongue, this time. "Let each stand in his place."

The International working class shall be the human race!" came out of every mouth in the barn, amplified in intensity and volume by the still-standing walls of The Hold Out. Appended by what Kumar felt was the ghost of outlaw Sam Pickering.

But as from the other Sam, the one whom Kumar wanted to be part of this Movement most, there came nothing. Sam Longmore walked out of the barn without so much as looking at Kumar. Or anyone else.

An inner voice, perhaps that of Sam Pickering, informed Kumar that this was the most important night of his so far theoretical but not actively committed life. Sam Longmore was Kumar's only real mentor. Someone he could ask for advise who would give him an honest answer. Someone who knew how things really were, or who knew more than most fellow humans on the planet did. Someone who would remind Kumar when he was flying up towards the sky to reach higher aspirations, or dive bombing into a rock-hard abyss.

Kumar was on his own now. A man who was in charge of transforming the world. A lonely man who would share the celebrations with his crew if things went right, but would be forced to walk off the plank and tossed into the deep six if they didn't. An honored position, according to Kumar's heroic Grandfather and sell-out father, both of whom he could only see in dreams or nightmares, now. But there was one perk for this hard-earned 'sentence' to a life where Work would replace all play.

After the third singing of the Internationale, with three-part harmony now, Leona wrapped her arm around Kumar's waist, then kissed him. On the lips this time. She appended it with a smile of gratitude and, yes, the elusive interactional feeling that all humans need and never really understand, love.

CHAPTER 8

Mother Nature saw fit to delivery warm winter winds that didn't carry much snow to the high country where the Morgan-Richter Mining and Oil inadvertently had uncovered economically useless uranium in the mountain instead. The roads leading up to it remained free of ice as well as mud. It allowed even thin tread-less tires on overloaded trucks, wooden wheels on hastily repaired carts, and badly trimmed hoofs of draft horses to grip the ground without so much as a slip that would lead to a slide down the mountain. It also allowed for the rapid building of the clandestine capital of the New American Empire coordinated by President Morgan and King Richter, and kept operational by very selected guests, some known to the working stiffs everywhere else, some not.

The workers Kumar hired to build the main meeting hall and adjacent lodge, with all of its elaborate indoor and outdoor trimming, completed the job faster than any barn-raising in the history of the county. Morgan and Richter's dollars got more work out of the selected wage slaves on Kumar's list than any other enterprise they started. Indeed, as Morgan and Richter saw it, Mother Nature and the common man were both slaves subject to their whims now. Such, of course, affirmed that God was on their side, without having to be paid off with any more contributions to any Church or Catholic Charity. However, the two local moguls who sought to be National Monarchs didn't realize that Queen in the making Melissa Bullock had her own plans to be Empress.

The moralistic drama and, depending on one's perspective, comedy of ironies, began on Armistice Day, otherwise known to the kids who chose to use their history books as something to wipe their asses with rather than feed their brains as November 11. Kumar's colorfully dysfunctional Comrades in what was, legally anyway, a crime were still skeptical about how tricking Blue River moguls Morgan and Richter and their special high-level tycoons from cities that had more people than cattle into doing the Right thing. They arrived at noon in limousines as black as the oil that made them able to drive them. They were adorned with gold paint, which blinded anyone who dared to look at them with an upright head. Among the chauffeured passengers was a plethora of brightly shining jewels in the form of cufflinks, tie pins, and canes. The latter were carried like swagger sticks stained to a deep brown red varnish hue with the blood, sweat, and tears of those they were broken in on. They all seemed impressed with the meeting hall constructed of freshly varnished wood featuring Greco-Roman bronze trimmings as well as the barrage of well-mannered, impeccably dressed, hunchbacked, more brawn than rebellions brains local servants with bowed heads who took their over-packed suitcases to their rooms.

Morgan, then Richter, decked out in freshly bought suits costing more than the locals' clothing store was worth, greeted each of the men of power and influence with a hearty handshake of equality as well as reverence as they entered the main meeting hall for lunch. He reminded them that there would be ample female entertainment after the completion of business at the hotel in town. Melissa Bullock was clad in a low-cut dress borrowed from the most attended courtesan at said hotel, with extra layers of makeup to hide the crow's feet around her eyes. She provided even the most hideously ugly guests with tailor-made compliments on their most valued physical attributes with Morgan and Richter's silent approval. She interspersed such with praise for what the guest in question had done to make America great again, secretly cajoling hints of secret plans from each of them as to how they were going to make themselves even greater. A clean-shaven, respectfully suited Kumar noted it all from his position as attaché to Morgan and Richter was voiced when out of range of their ears.

The names and affiliations of the attendees were equally impressive as the gold imprinted cards on their assigned places at the oversized, overweighing, and over-polished oak dining table inside the meeting hall. They included none other than K. Richard Ranselhoff, director of the Eastern Pacific Railroad, U.R. MacDonald, President of Western Atlantic Oil, F.U. Kuntsler, Founder of North American Textiles, and I.B. Younger, CEO of Imperial Steel.

Leona, clad in a tight fitting earth brown leather-wool dress with just enough fringes to make it seem to be authentic, assimilated 'Injun', with a large crucifix around her neck, came by the table. She adjusted the outfits of the white gloved waitresses charged with placing cigars, writing implements, paper, and the finest glasses for drinking berry wine available in front of the overly first name initialed royalty who would sit in front of them. She was assisted by two other ladies who volunteered for this 'front line' duty so that other women would be spared being killed, or worse. But their bravery did not come with a knowledge of fashion sense for the occasion.

"Your breasts are uneven, 'gentlemen,'" Leona said as she adjusted the artificial breasts under bras worn by Wilson and Dubois, whose faces were clean-shaven for the first time in a year. "And you both need more lipstick." She reached into her pocket and made their chapped lips a deeper shade of red. Such was necessary so as to draw attention away from the dark brown foundation over the rest of their face and exposed skin on their arms and neck. It was essential for Wilson and Du Bois to appear to be servants from the inferior gender as well as a 'subhuman' colored race. "And if we are going to pull this off, particularly with both of you observing clinical signs in the fat cat lab rats who will be in here before you can say 'George Armstrong Custer is a pampered, self-absorbed, Mama's boy with delusions of grandeur,' which he was, try smiling and waltzing around the room, like Sister Paul there."

Leona discreetly pointed Lady Wilson and Dubois to Father Smith, who was in black face and a conservatively designed dress. He was setting up the buffet table for the Power Meeting with a gracious dance in his step, a musical lilt of his wrists, as well as a delicate movement of his fingers when handing the silverware. It was culminated by his adjusting his curly shoulder-length wig with the fourth and fifth digit of his fingers.

"It's an act," Leona assured Wilson and Dubois regarding the 'sexy progressive Nun'.

"Was it an act when Sister Paula presented herself as Father Paul, or when Father Paul was pretending to be Sister Paula since he arrived in this town?" Dubois grunted through ruby red lips. "Which explains a few things about him and his past, and why he is here. which---"

"----Are not important now," Wilson interjected, pointing to the door to the lobby opening up. The procession of Captains, and if they had anything to do with it, Generals of Industry, strolled into the room like Presidential Royalty on their way to take their assigned seats at the round table. "We have to be sure these gentlemen get exactly what's coming to them, pharmacologically and otherwise," the Doctor, whose job it was to help dose and clinically assess the lab rats who owned and decided who got into so many universities and medical schools. So far, anyway.

"'Gentlemen,' you call these robber barons, thieves and scoundrels?" Dubois added. "Gentlemen who broke so many of us. Who will we train to do what we tell them to? Gentleman who will lick my boots! Gentlemen..."

"---And lady," Leona interjected in the middle of the rant by the beaten but far from defeated man of many trades, as Melissa came into the hall. She lifted the name tag of one of the male participants off the table at the opposite end of

Morgan's position, then crumbled it like a squashed bug still grasping for life. She then sat down at the table with the rest of the men. "Yes. Mellissa. A lady who---" Leona continued.

"---Is in this room by the guests' request, and obviously not the hosts'," Wilson noted as he and his lead-gloved 'sister in crime' Dubois proceeded towards the table containing the first bottle of Uranium-spiked wine, which would be poured into the glasses on the table. To the exact proportions of the toasters' body weight.

Leona's third eye sensed Mellissa's stare at her. The descendent of European and American Royalty smiled at the ancestor of First Nations Warriors, Sages, and Chiefs in the manner of a Queen to her most willing subject. Leona returned the gesture, with an accentuated bow, but 'Queen Millissa knew that this First Nations was on the warpath. Each woman, of course, knew that secret agendas were so often the ones that came to pass more often than those stated out right. But in the meantime, it still was a man's world.

With bowed heads and, to the varying extents, wiggling asses, the blackfaced 'waitresses' served food made appealing to the palate by Mary Steiner's cooking skills and selectively psychoactive by Leona's expertise in pharmacology. Leana returned to their station near the kitchen, taking on the demeaner of a decorative, silent, but always watching totem pole. Morgan, at the head of the more rectangular than round table, stood up on his two underused feet and raised his glass of 'power berry' wine, thinking, of course, that there was more brain-expanding extract in his glass than anyone else's.

"A toast, gentlemen!" he proclaimed to his fellow penis bearers, with joy. "And Lady," he continued, to Mellissa, by necessity, as he saw more than one of those penises grow bigger in the presence of the Lady who invited herself to the table. "To this first annual Western conference of us, the best of the best. Who can be the Greatest of the Great if we… take more control of what we control already."

"Together. A Supermen," as handsome as Morgan was homely, Richter added with a big, bold baritone voice that echoed around the room.

"And superwomen," Lady Mellissa reminded Richter, her, for the moment anyway, husband-to-be.

"Smart Superwomen," Ranselhoff proclaimed. He smiled at Melissa so wide that the waxed tips of his handlebar mustache nearly touched his ears. "With memories as great as any Superman."

"Expanding their horizons, like supermen," offered Kuntsler, the German immigrant who built his first fortune selling arms to the Kaiser in the Great War and his second treasure chest doing business with the Allies after America joined the War to End All Wars.

"Confident. Proud. Never doubting themselves," declared Younger in an unapologetic aristocratic Georgian plantation owner accent, one that was passed down to him by his Dixie ancestors, along with his grandfather's Confederate Colt which he, according to rumor anyway, had been used to kill his way to into acquiring as many counties in Colorado as his grandfather had slaves.

"Takers of power, influence and wealth," Highland Scot born McDonald echoed from a double-sized mouth rolling his r's so loud that one could feel the room rumble under your feet. "Strong winners who are, because we are good Christian men, caretakers of the weak. And disciplinarians of them when such is necessary."

"With magical abilities that will spring from special centers and the good earth around it like this, to be on top of the top," Morgan proclaimed, anticipating his ability to not only be partners but masters of these moguls after the first glass of power berry wine. "With the help and those few talented people temporarily on the bottom, that helped make that magic possible," he related and confessed, pointing to Leona and Kumar, who were at the positions assigned to them just outside the kitchen door.

Morgan invited and commanded Kumar and Leona to pour a glass of wine for themselves from the 'magic bottle' from which he himself got a larger portion than all of his guests. Leona picked up the glasses next to them as they stood by the kitchen door. Leona smiled, bowed, then poured the (as Morgan thought it was) 'brain and balls promoting elixir into two glasses, half-filling them. She handed one to Kumar, who lifted it up to his exceedingly generous patron mentor and mark.

"Yes. With this nectar of the gods!" mortal Morgan, anticipating that he would soon be equal to the god Zeus, proclaimed. "Which we drink as gods."

"And goddesses!" Melissa insisted, in the manner of a mother who was both taskmaster to an errant child and mistress to a man who considered adultery as a required act of strength rather than a weakness of character.

"Yes," Morgan conceded.

With that, Melissa sipped her wine, like a lady, as the men gulped theirs down as the more assertive gender. Thankfully, the men were more concerned with looking at Lady Melissa than Injun Princess Leona, or Squire Kumar. It allowed the two latter Comrades to discreetly pour the contents of their uranium-spiked wine into spittoons that would be cleaned out in short order.

"Yes, gods and goddesses, on day one anyway," Leona whispered to fellow commoner Kumar as the royals toasted each other yet again, and as predicted, led by Richter. "And as for days two, three, and five," a more confident than ever Leona said to an abruptly cautious Kumar.

CHAPTER 9

Leona had insisted on dosing Morgan and his guests with uranium-laced wine and food. Comfortable hot baths were scheduled for all the moguls after their so-called "hard day" devising new ways to distance themselves from the planet's "commoners" in both wealth and social prestige. She claimed the sedation had to occur so their minds wouldn't notice how their brains were being manipulated, much like what had been done to her people in the latter half of the previous century.

Wilson monitored their clinical signs with meticulous care. "Sister Paula" assured the guests that their lightheadedness wasn't due to losing brain cells, but simply a side effect of the increased elevation—and of being brought closer to Heaven with every humanitarian decision they made regarding their fortunes.

With a hoarse voice—blamed on a new version of the Spanish Flu circulating in the valley—Dubois assured Morgan and the others that the new strain, which was ravaging the commoners in town, would not affect self-made kings and queens. It was, he claimed, Mother Nature's way of culling the inferior population while preserving those destined to rule from the mountaintop.

Before the grand opening of the new Gentleman's Club in the high country—and in the three days leading up to the banquet—Kumar had managed to cajole his way from Morgan's attaché to his junior partner and most trusted advisor. More trusted even than Richter. The honest-as-the-day-is-long (at least in summer) Sikh cowboy had also secured a similar arrangement with Richter.

By the fourth evening of this power summit—the power meeting of power meetings—Morgan, Richter, the other gentlemen, and Mellissa gathered again for dinner. They had spent the day crafting increasingly unworkable plans to turn their collective and individual territories into empires. As usual, Morgan began with a toast. But this evening, the master planner—who could usually think five chess moves ahead—didn't even know where the board was, or whether his pieces were white or black.

"A toast, after a productive day of saving America by..." he began boldly, before his eyes turned glassy. Turning to Richter, he muttered, "What did we do yesterday and earlier today?" believing he was whispering, though even Mary in the kitchen heard his confused voice.

"Something great and... I hope productive for America," Richter replied, his lips trembling with terror. "Our America," he added, trying to convince himself. "Right, Mister Patel?" he asked, addressing Kumar as "Mister" for the first time.

"I wrote down everything you and the other gentlemen—and lady—decided," Kumar said calmly, trying to draw his two 'bosses' back together. "We'll need your signatures verified to make it official." He motioned to Leona, who brought over a briefcase filled with newly signed transfers of property and rights.

"Yeah… I've signed so many things today that one of my three arms is tired," slurred Kunstler, double-visioned and dazed. "What did I sign, Emmmersttttton?" he asked out of the side of his mouth, directing the question to Morgan.

"What my trusted apprentice, Mister Patel, drew up," Morgan proclaimed, swaying like a drunk king in a sandbox rather than a castle.

"Important papers, based on your own instructions," Kumar added, assuring Ranselhoff and the others as Leona presented the documents. "All signed."

"And some that I composed," Leona whispered to Kumar. "And some that—"

"—Are blank," Kumar finished in a whisper, impressed. "Which we'll both fill in later," he added with a grunt, forcing a smile on the men. "Which will—"

"Make them as broke as they made us," Leona finished, in Lakota, flashing a smile of delight at the men.

"I nay kin! What did that lassie bampot say?" McDonald asked in a thick Scottish brogue, paranoia rising like bile. It echoed the terror his 'hero' uncle must have felt at Little

Bighorn when he realized just how many Indigenous warriors had shown up for karmic payback.

Ranselhoff leaned even farther back in his chair, puffing on his cigar with an uncharacteristically carefree grin. "Something… profound. And… magical. Like what's in these cigars that makes me... less competitive. And more... hungry for this really great food," he said, suddenly lunging forward to dip his fingers into a bowl of berry jam. He licked the bowl and his fingers with more passion than any overpaid hooker, beggar, or demoted employee had ever licked his boots or toe-jam.

Younger, a fruit-hating "meat and potatoes only" man, finally set down his cigar and reached for his allotted berry topping with a spoon, mostly right side up. "Yes. Those who dine together, liberate the world together—cooperatively," said the grandson of a former slave owner, who had just unknowingly signed away ownership of hundreds of black, white, and yellow-skinned 'employees.'

"Made possible by me putting the uranium in the food," Leona whispered to Kumar.

"And me putting my special weed in their cigars to make them eat it," Kumar reminded her. "Not that it tastes as good as they think."

"And if they eat too much, too fast," Leona warned.

"We schleps, serfs, and slaves take this country back— sooner than later," Kumar replied. "Giving some of it back to my people, who were here long before they crossed the oceans, 'Mister' Patel."

"Sure," Kumar said, unsure how to address Leona this time. She kept changing her preferences. "That's what I said. But these lab rats need to lose their edge. Their will to—"

"—Do or say anything. With or to anyone," Dr. Professor Leona interjected. She pointed to Younger, now completely detached from everything and everyone. Then to Kunstler, who stared blankly at the vegetables, meat, and potatoes in front of him, none of which he seemed to recognize. His stomach grumbled.

Mellissa, who had strategically placed herself next to Kunstler—the richest of the barons—for two days straight, leaned in. "I.B.—I mean, Isiah Bentley… You're hungry, but you're not eating. Thirsty, but you don't drink. And…" With trembling hands guided by strong will rather than the invisible puppet masters controlling the men's limbs, she slipped her hand between Kunstler's legs, giving a rhythmic, gentle rub. But unlike other times, the structure beneath her touch softened rather than hardened.

"Nothing there," Kumar heard her mutter, his keen ears confirmed by his recently honed lip-reading skills. "From the only man in this room who had the balls and brains to fuck these wimps economically who—" She continued, no longer caring who heard her. Her eyes locked onto the document Kunstler had signed, draining his fortune into the hands of the poor and indigent. Then, she saw the catatonic glaze in his eyes, the dumb, blissful smile on his face.

"So, the once-great Kunstler who signed away his fortune to 'the less fortunate' as an investment is now a…"

"—Nothing. In a world where nothing matters," Younger intoned, sounding like a prophet in some wonderland behind his glassy stare. "But not to nothings like me," he added, abruptly feeling like the shit being flushed down the toilet, rather than the asshole doing the flushing.

Leona smiled, satisfied to see Mellissa alone and frustrated. Mellissa scanned the room—men disconnected from each other, from themselves, from the very idea of who they were supposed to be. She stood up. As she passed by Kumar and Leona, she stumbled.

Kumar offered a hand. She refused it with more stubbornness than he'd seen in any woman—even Leona. For the first time, Mellissa was at the bottom of the socio-economic ladder. But unlike the men, she was aware of who had put her there.

"My legs just went limp!" she snapped, glaring into Kumar's eyes. "My brain's fine. It will tell my legs where to go."

"Or to the poor house," Kumar muttered to himself, celebrating a rare day when clever right triumphed over economic might.

"But not the fucking Nunnery!" Mellissa shouted as she pushed herself to her feet and stumbled out the door.

Wilson approached, his stride a blend of sashay and stoic pride.

"So… you don't need me to be a waitress or nurse anymore?" he asked his two 'supervisors.' "I can go back to being a doctor? A male doctor?"

"With a pharmacy stocked with everything your patients need," Kumar replied, handing Wilson documents signed by Morgan and Richter, confirming their "donation" to his clinic. "Everything they need."

"And more of what they want…" Leona added, placing a blank sheet of gold-embedded stationery bearing Morgan's signature in Wilson's other hand. "Such as…" She scribbled a few "donations" on the page. Wilson's ruby-red lips curled into a smile that was both pleased and powerful—both manly and womanly.

"And if you want," Leona added, "after you're done experimenting as Doctor Willimina… a new dress. Shoes. A wig."

"One that wasn't taken by scalping some heiress," Kumar added, nodding toward the doors. Outside sat Melissa, crumpled, sobbing like a lone peasant who had lost home, bread, and family.

"Right?" he asked Leona.

"We'll see," she replied. Her real thoughts, feelings, and intentions stayed hidden behind eyes that had seen more horror in her real life as a Western Indian than Kumar had known in his relatively sheltered life as an East Indian.

CHAPTER 10

Christmas came early that year.

With all the legal documents signed—and the signers now confined to mental wards, unable to recall their own names or former roles as robber barons—Santa Kumar and company made sure that everything the rich had taken from the poor was returned.

As for explaining this turn of events to the people of Blue River, Dubois—the new owner of the coal mines where he worked harder than many of the men under him—told the townsfolk there'd been another Stock Market crash, one only the rich had access to. That, he said, explained his sudden wealth.

Doc Wilson's clinic, now fully stocked with effective medications, was finally able to offer care based on need, entirely free of charge. When asked why, he told his curious patients that a virus was going around—one that devoured a part of the cerebral cortex responsible for compassion, making people greedy, cruel, and oblivious to the universal law of "what goes around comes around." He even gave it a Latin name.

Father Smith preached that Jesus had appeared to Morgan, Richter, and the other moguls in a vision, and that their souls were undergoing "reconstruction" through a mix of prayer and medication while in confinement.

Lady Melissa, now a limping laundress, had traded her high heels and insults for washbins and humility. Once known for seducing rich men and kicking the downtrodden when they were already down, she now scrubbed clothes beside the very women she had scorned. Leona claimed that Melissa had taken a spill while skiing in the hills—an accident that jostled her brain and her hindlimbs alike.

Kumar was elected Comrade Mayor, largely because he didn't want the job. When asked why he accepted it, he simply said, "Karma's a bitch that comes to bite you in the ass." He hoped his words would serve as a warning to the people who now owned the homes, farms, and stores once seized by the bank: don't become as greedy, cruel, and ignorant as those who came before.

Unlike the so-called "golden times" in Blue River—when gold, silver, or oil had been discovered by hard-working citizens but hoarded by the privileged—this new era didn't care about skin color, country, or state of origin. A new law, needing no sheriff to enforce it, banned all signs excluding Irish, Mexicans, migrant Okies, Indians, Blacks, or "Chinks" from honest work. Wages were now fair.

No one dared put up signs denying women men's jobs—maybe out of fear of Leona's wrath.

Father Smith's Hallelujah Café now operated out of Morgan's former five-star restaurant. A sign in the window read:

"All you need to eat. All day, every day. Pay what you can—if you can."

The communal grocery store followed the same model, selling goods both local and imported. No one went hungry. No one was cold. No one lacked shelter.

But there were still a few things that needed adjusting.

"How long should we—and our trusted Comrades—keep them like this?" asked Doc Wilson, his beard grown back, as he and Kumar watched Morgan and Richter take their daily walk outside the expanded hospital. Morgan looked vacant; Richter slapped himself as if trying to remember who he used to be.

Patients Ranselhoff, Younger, and McDonald were being escorted into a car bound for other treatment centers run by Wilson's most trusted colleagues.

"And how long do we keep them disconnected from their former selves?" Doc added.

"Until we-or your smart research buddies in Denver—find a biological cure for greed, cruelty, evil, and stupidity," Kumar replied.

"Socrates said the cure for all evil is knowledge," Wilson mused. "As well as wisdom and—"

"—Be sure they don't get kidney problems," Leona interrupted, having once again snuck up on them "Injun-style," her moccasins silent on the pavement.

"And keep Morgan and Richter away from her," Wilson added, nodding toward Melissa Bullock, who was vigorously scrubbing laundry beside the very women she had once dismissed—and the town's working girls, whom she had once looked down upon.

"So, without those men—Morgan, Richter, and the rest—Lady Melissa really is broke," Kumar observed.

"When it comes to personal money, she always was," Wilson said. "She lived off 'allowances' from whatever man she was trying to trap into marriage—without ever risking pregnancy herself, of course. But now, being the only woman in this socio-biological experiment of ours, she's an interesting lab rat. One who may cause problems down the line."

"And you know this, Doc, because…?" Leona pressed.

"Doctor–patient confidentiality," Wilson muttered, his back straightening, his eyes avoiding hers. "Some rules we still have to obey. Even if they're—"

"—Un-American!" came a familiar voice.

"And illegal!" barked ex-Sheriff Johnston, still in his U.S. Army uniform. His voice cut through the air like a blade.

"Which all of this probably is," he added.

"Maybe, Captain Johnston," Kumar replied, glancing at the new captain's bars on Johnston's tunic—and the torn-off colonel flaps.

"And if you make any more false accusations, Sergeant or Private Johnston," Leona warned, glaring at the red-faced bully,

"I'll have you know I was a decorated Indian fighter!" Johnston snapped. "Special assignment during the Yaqui revolt in Mexico, back in '26!" he added, turning toward Doc Wilson, who remained polite only by professional habit.

"The history books will call it a revolution," Kumar said quietly.

"And record who assigned you to go there," Leona added, appending the comment with one of her accusatory looks—the kind that made you feel she knew your deepest, most incriminating secrets, even when she didn't.

Johnston huffed and puffed like an outsmarted, proud-cut colt denied the chance to kick the crap out of his trainer.

"We'll see about that!" he grunted in frustration. "But I know things about all of you—or I can make them up and have people believe them, and—"

"—Second Lieutenant Johnston!" Kumar heard from behind Johnston—a voice he was more than pleasantly aware of.

Colonel Oliver, the first Native American in Colorado's Army Reserve to hold that rank, barked at his now-subordinate officer from atop a military truck filled with soldiers of lower rank.

"Of course," Johnston mumbled, still gripping his pride like a fraying rope.

"Of course, what?" Oliver snapped, pointing at the silver eagles on his shoulders—formerly Johnston's—now earned as part of the de-segregation order drunkenly signed by a uranium-berry-wine-intoxicated Morgan and Richter.

"Of course, sir," Johnston grumbled.

"You mean—sirs, I suggest strongly," Oliver corrected, gesturing toward a dirt-poor Irish immigrant Captain and a Black Major—both of whom had once been a Private and a Corporal under Johnston's command.

"Alright! Of course, sirs!" Johnston barked, pulling his rifle over his shoulder and climbing into the truck with the rest of his troops.

The detachment—once dispatched by federal and corporate moguls to keep out American migrants, Mexicans, and political dissidents—left Blue River. Their new orders: build houses for displaced families in nearby counties, whose homes had been bulldozed after foreclosure by Morgan's satellite banks.

Leona and Kumar shared a smile—genuine, broad, hard-earned. But, as always in matters both medical and moral, Doc Wilson's face bore caution.

"Just remember," he said, voice low but firm, addressing both Leona and Kumar. "Fugam gloria est," the self-appointed healer of body, mind, and soul proclaimed, before turning and walking away, leaving it to them to heed or ignore his advice.

"What did he say?" Kumar asked.

"'Glory is fleeting,'" Leona translated, her voice distant but knowing. She recalled—no doubt—the buffalo days of her people, when mastery over horse and herd brought triumph over rival tribes… until it didn't.

Then she turned to Kumar, ready to share the more profound lesson they were, hopefully, learning together.

"Maybe something you remember from that past life in Rome you keep dreaming about," she said. "Where we drove the rich mad and helped the empire fall—only to be replaced by…"

"…Something better. This time," Kumar declared. "And while we're quoting the ancients to sound learned, something from one of your heroes and Al Einstein's: Isaac Newton…"

He paused, drawing a breath.

"'Energy, once created, is never destroyed,'" he said—in Lakota—his tongue struggling to shape vowels and consonants that belonged to no language he'd spoken before.

Leona scratched her chin, then looked deep into Kumar, through him, even.

"I'm impressed," she finally said. "And you even did it with... sort of understandable pronunciation."

Kumar gave a playful bow and thanked her in his best pre-rehearsed academic German, Russian, French, Spanish, and Ancient Greek—feeling, for once, genuinely proud of himself.

"But," Leona added, cocking her head with a grin, "as the white-nigger Scot hiding in my family tree back in 1789, Angus William McDermott, used to say: If ye dae guid th'day, ye hae tae dae better th'mora."

Kumar chuckled, catching the meaning: If you do good today, you have to do better tomorrow.

"Nae probs," he replied, matching her accent as best he could.

Then, from his breast pocket, Kumar pulled a joint filled with his signature mellow weed.

"Without that," Leona snapped, pointing at it. "We're launching a new social experiment here—requires a clear head."

She softened. "Please."

Kumar considered her words, then nodded and tucked the joint back into his pocket.

"But it does make me feel good," he admitted.

Leona leaned in and kissed him softly. Then she pulled back, her eyes giving him another kind of kiss—of trust, of admiration, of something unspoken but growing.

"That makes me feel better," said Comrade Mayor Kumar, smiling wider than any high the weed had ever given him.

Cheers rose from the town's citizens—less fancy in clothes than before, but richer in dignity. They cheered not a ruler, but a coordinator. Not a mayor, but a comrade.

And Leona embraced him again.

Yes, glory was fleeting. But to not seize the day and savor it would be an insult—not only to the many gods folded within the Great Spirit—but a disservice to the humanity it serves... and is served by.

CHAPTER 11

It didn't take long for the news about the town as well as surrounding county, in Colorado that had no police force, no REAL Mayor in charge of the citizenry, no hunger, no unemployment, no homelessness, no newspapers that increased their readership by telling emotionally charge lies rather than the bare bones truth, to reach the populated centers that urban dwellers still called the 'important' part of the world. One such location, of course, was New York City, a town of 6 million souls whose consciousness and travels, rightly or wrongly, seldom went west of New Jersey. But despite the white lies of hope offered by Priests on Sunday morning to nearly penniless parishioners and on Saturday night over the radio by politicians who needed votes from the huddled masses to be re-elected to their still high-paying jobs in Washington and Albany, the gap between the have-nots and haves was never greater.

One of those privileged, overly 'haves' sat comfortably in his office in the top story of his still maintained and, thanks to the Cops and sometimes Federal troops down below on the street, not bombed by 'Commie Anarchists' building in lower Manhattan. R.B. Wentworth rotated his pot-bellied but somehow handsomely clad in a brown tweed suit torso towards his window. He gazed down at the American flags flying proudly on every one of the office buildings while ordinary citizens, some of whom had lost an arm, leg, or eye fighting to defend it overseas in the Great War, begged for food from those who still had matching shoes with intact soles on their feet.

"The way it is," the double-chinned, immaculately bearded and neatly combed back brown-grey haired Boston Blue blood who had not only survived but, due to tips from undisclosed sources, flourished after the 1929 Stock Market crash said to his guest with a baritone voice that echoed from his double chin. He felt himself to be both God's and America's personally assigned prophet atop the brick-and-mortar Mount Sinai. He was born to a well-off family in Boston. Due to luck and some cunning, he was able to marry his way into a richer one in Long Island. His wife died a year later, leaving him the seeds for his next fortune. Recalling all of the above, he took another puff from his Cuban cigar. "Yes, the gap between those of us who have and those who don't," he said as he looked out the window again. A Cop pulled away another emaciated one-handed War veteran unwashed hobo, this one wearing a Red Star on his cap, for 'three squares and a cot' in jail, with, of course, a well-deserved beating beforehand. "The way it is here in the East," the gambler who, by various means and divinely passed on good fortune, never lost any toss of the dice in any game he played, noted with a sense of righteousness and glee as was his habit, and passion. "And almost every place in the West," he continued, gazing at the smog emerging from his factories in New Jersey. It added an 'interesting' color of grey to what had usually been a clear blue sky a generation ago. "But not apparently, where you came from," Wentworth noted to his guest, picking up a copy of the Colorado People's Herald, its main office in Blue River.

Wentworth waddled his underused legs towards his desk. He retrieved a bottle of 'wildberry' brandy specially mailed to him from that location from 'an admiring friend'. He then took two glasses from his gold-trimmed, oak cabinet, pouring an equal portion for himself and his honored guest.

"Special and very expensive berry brandy," he noted regarding the elixir that smelled so fragrant to his oversized nostrils. "Which, according to the manufacturer, has special herbs that give 'pleasure the palate and special power to the innovative all American innovated soul'," he read on the label bearing the likeness of a philosophical East Indian Western Mountain man and the most beautiful portrait of 'Princess Pocahontas' he ever imagined possible.

For reasons Wentworth couldn't figure out, the US Army Officer seated in front of his desk refused to imbibe the brandy. And even more to his surprise, when Wentworth tried to sip a portion of it, his guest abruptly slapped the glass out of his hand, grabbed hold of the bottle, spit on the images of the people on it, and smashed it to smithereens inside the trash can. Then, said guest calmly walked back to his chair and plopped his ass down on it.

"A fellow highly decorated veteran who is a zealous tea toddler," Wentworth noted, gazing yet again and the red, white, and blue ribboned clanking medals adorning most of the left side of his tunic. "I can honor that, as you honor me, by telling me alone

about what is happening in the go-nowhere landlocked Colorado town that is making a big splash on both coasts." Wentworth perused the stack of legal documents, newspaper clippings, and affidavits on his desk that the Sergeant from the other side of the Continental Divide had come to deliver to his hands, and no one else's. "So this is what you claim is happening in this illegal, immoral, and, more importantly, very un-American social experiment in Blue River. But before I take this to the board of boards in this always-going-somewhere town…" Lord Wentworth put down the papers, leaned back on his chair, and stared into the angrily determined, yet somehow conflicted, face of the soldier who had risked life and limb to have a private meeting with him. "Tell me why you are here, and tell me all of this, Sergeant…"

"Longmore," Sam, Kumar's former mentor-friend and now ideological enemy, said as he felt the tightness of the uniform he had put into the closet for safekeeping nearly 20 years ago. "Former Sergeant Sam Longmore."

"Who re-enlisted again, so my sources tell me. As a knight in shining yet tight-fitting armor, according to your service record," Wentworth mused at yet another button on Longmire's tunic, which was about to pop loose if he breathed any heavier. "Or perhaps a Judas, who---."

"Has to stop the new Jesuses in my town," Sam asserted, leaning forward across Wentworth's desk, his hand clenched in a fist. "Who doesn't know that redistributing wealth before its natural time is wrong and ultimately… destructive."

"Yes," Wentworth agreed, calmly. He reached for his cigar, igniting it with a gold-plated lighter. He blew smoke up into the air rather than into the face of the veteran from the other side of the tracks, whom he knew would have to establish a rapport with, for the sake of his well-being and maintaining the status quo of the country God had entrusted him to manage. "Because the commoner, especially in this country, is ignorant. Give the masses too much power and wealth too early, and they will become a destructive, anarchist mob. John Adams said that. But you say, or feel, something different."

Wentworth decided abruptly to blow smoke into Sam's face, which made him cough, but not shut up. "The common man is a noble man," the seasoned Western cowboy and former well-decorated veteran continued, calmly this time. "Because he knows that to be noble, he has to render unto Caesar that which is Caesar's. And a newly rich man, particularly one who has been poor, will turn into a corrupt, evil one. One who is worse than his former economic Master."

"Masters like me, Sergeant Longmore?" Wentworth challenged, utilizing his X-ray vision to see beyond the four layers of facades a man puts up. And to see to his real core and agenda, which, rightly or wrongly, few men, or women, were ever really aware of themselves. "Master like me, whom do you see as an economic and political necessity?" He aimed his oversized mouth at Sam to blow another blast of tobacco at the non-smoker. But instead, he puffed out a perfectly symmetrical circle of white smoke up to the ceiling.

"Yes," Sergeant Longmore replied. "Men like you are required to be Masters on top. Until a smooth, legal, and moral distribution of wealth happens at the bottom. As the REAL Jesus intended. Heaven on earth."

"And the saying that it's easier for a camel to get through the eye of a needle than a rich man to get into heaven, Sam?" Wentworth inquired, putting down his over-priced custom-blend Havana rolled stogie.

"Not true for rich men who help the poor, when they can, and should. Smartly, and

wisely," replied the bold Sergeant and apparently equally intelligent philosopher cowboy who wanted to return to the home he had exiled himself from when it was 'home' again. "Someone has ta be in charge of the money, just like someone has ta be in charge of the horse that moves the cattle. Right?" he continued in diction more in keeping with his real identity and agenda.

"Yes indeed," Wentworth said as slowly as he could, so as to let the thought incubating in his mind take final form and be voiced without interruption from anyone else. "By blockading the cattle that are about to stampede the town," he continued as he glanced to the Western horizon beyond

New Jersey through his window. He visualized the tailor-made-for-the-customer (or mark) metaphor. "Or run off a cliff. Like…we did in Russia back in 1918 and 19…" Images of the Big Wide Open in the Wild East from nearly 20 years ago ushered into Wentworth's mind, pulling his vision away to the medals he acquired, by various means of course, when he was in service to his country as a high ranking officer in the Army rather than a civilian on his way up the political and economic ladder back home. "The international and mostly American-funded expeditionary force we used against the Bolsheviks after tossing the Kaiser out of office in Germany didn't work as well as we planned."

"Yes," Sam said, recalling his extended period of military service that he didn't tell anyone in Colorado about. "But the blockade of Russia kept the godless, armed, and radical Communists locked and hungry inside their own experiment."

"Which would have destroyed that experiment if we were funded better. Not shackled by deluded soft-hearted politicians in Washington and London, Sam,"

"Or if we were distracted by the Spanish Flu, which killed more people than cannon-fire, bayonets, or trench-foot. Or us being exhausted after winning 'the Great War' in the trenches, which everybody in one way or another lost, Major Wentworth," Sam said, noting the rank on the photos of Wentworth in uniform behind his desk.

"Yes," former Major Wentworth noted. He felt a rush of sincerity down his spine as he crossed himself in the manner his Catholic mother had taught him to do at home. Such was an 'insurance policy' that he used when asking God to look after the slain enlisted men who died on the front after enthusiastically carrying out orders passed down to him from the Colonels and Generals. "But this time our weapons are economic…and very, very legal, Sergeant, and as I DO have something to say about it, Captain Longmore."

"And these weapons and strategies are moral as well as legal, Colonel Wentworth?" the patriotic and religious cowboy inquired.

It wasn't the first time a trusted and specially brought in subordinate had posed such a question to Wentworth. As such, he provided his answer in a pre-rehearsed manner, which he used in the last 100 deals he made with such well-meaning Judases. "Our strategy and methods are as moral as possible in a world God assigned to endure, survive, and, with enough American ingenuity, transform."

Wentworth appended the deal by pouring cups of tea for himself and Sam. He proposed a toast. "To…transforming America to what it should and is destined to be. So help us God!"

It was a toast that no true American who still believed in Jesus, or who knew how to control those who did, could argue with.

CHAPTER 12

The last letter Kumar's heroic—yet historically unrecorded—grandfather, Arjun, wrote before he was executed by the British Army had remained unopened for decades. It was finally sent to Kumar by his father, likely because he knew it was time his son considered its contents. The letter read:

Enlightenment—and the masochistic madness that accompanies it—skips a generation.

You will die a coward's death, slowly, if you follow in the footsteps of your economically successful father, who published magazines and books filled with whatever his American patrons and purchasers wanted to read.

The greatest contributions you make to the world are appreciated and implemented only after you die.

Never believe everything you read in print.

The most painful way to live is to be too comfortable.

It was those final two points that hit Kumar the hardest—and rang the truest—as he stood on Main Street in Blue River in his new role as Mayor.

He was receiving the latest batch of newspapers, offloaded from delivery trucks that had once been used to export hobos, Mexicans, and Okie migrants out of the state. On that crisp morning, Kumar was dressed in the third outfit approved by the town council for a man of his position: Philosopher-King-Mayor. The outfit included jeans with no tears, a shirt with intact pockets, boots unsoiled by cowshit, and a wide-brimmed "going-to-meeting" cowboy hat unsullied by either angry cattle or angry rainclouds.

Still, Kumar couldn't shake a growing unease. His new job felt far too easy compared to his previous callings: managing cattle, tutoring both gifted and ordinary children, building barns, and being—at times—the horse himself. He allowed himself a brief read of the front-page stories from the Denver Gazette and other city papers—cities that had once been rural, now urbanized. All of them covered what they referred to as the "Socialist Experiment" in Blue River.

Kumar gasped—first in disbelief, then in anger—as he read articles and government letters reporting "rampant" infections: deadly bacteria in crops, viruses in people, and exotic diseases in cattle. The accusations were absurd. Yet proof that these lies were believed came—on the hoof.

Jake and Buddy returned with the town's prize cattle— healthy, strong, co-owned by the citizenry of Blue River. They had taken them to market in nearby counties and to the railheads bound for Denver, Chicago, and San Francisco. But they came back—rejected, branded diseased. The diagnoses included anthrax, hoof-and-mouth disease, even afflictions Kumar had never heard of—"confirmed" by university autopsies and lab tests in Denver, the very institutions Kumar had once dreamed of attending.

Meanwhile, from the opposite side of town, trucks and wagons returned as well—loaded with prime wheat, potatoes, cheese, rice, and barrels of brewed wine, some of it, admittedly, spiked with uranium for "special buyers." Some carts were still full. Others were half-burned.

"This is bullshit!" Kumar growled to Leona as she approached. "We have the healthiest cattle, best crops, and fittest people in the goddamn state—maybe the whole country!"

"Reading is believing," Leona replied dryly, helping herself to a toxic dose of easily recognizable lies in crisp black-and-white print—lies that echoed across every "All the News That's Fit to Wipe Your Ass With" newspaper.

"Charming fairy tales," she added, with a cynical grimace. "From the same reporters whose fathers claimed we were bloodthirsty savages who scalped nuns and feasted on white Christian children after torching their churches and farms."

"—Hey! These cattle are supposed to be sold! Somewhere else! Anywhere else!" Kumar yelled to Buddy as he drove the herd back into the holding corrals.

"No one wants cattle with anthrax or hoof-in-mouth disease!" Buddy yelled back.

"Or rinderpest," Leona noted calmly, reading aloud from one of the articles. "A disease that only occurs in Africa… and hasn't existed there in thirty years."

"But the wheat? The potatoes? Barley? Corn? Even the hay? They won't let us sell anything!" Kumar barked, panic rising in his throat. "Half of it was sent back, and the other half they burned! In a country starving for food—for both people and livestock!"

Leona flipped to a newspaper from Laramie, owned by a New York publishing house. She put on a thick Irish brogue and smiled wickedly. "Ah, me ladies. Seems the taters and all our lovely agricultural crops—fine-tastin' berries included—caught a wee bit of Phytophthora infestans. That nasty bug, mostly spelled right here, which apparently came to our God-fearing country courtesy of well-organized Irish Anarchist Communists."

"Anarchists don't organize anything!" Kumar roared.

"International anarchists who snuck into the country illegally," Leona added, now dropping the Gaelic flourish. "And made their way into Colorado with help from…"

"Godless Communists," Father Smith said, walking by, quoting the article without missing a beat.

"And the tractors we paid for?" Kumar demanded, directing his question at the heavens, his fellow citizens, and the Great Spirit who had inspired this "social experiment" in the first place. "Tractors—so we can feed everyone, including anti-Communist Christians after church on Sundays and every damn day of the week. So no more horses are worked to death pulling a plow!"

"The bulls and federal troops at the railhead said we should get 'em from Comrade Stalin," Buddy offered as he dismounted his sweat-soaked horse. He led the weary steed to the trough for water and rinsed the caked sweat, dust, and likely tears from his face.

"And the medical supplies?" Kumar asked, eyes narrowing as another truck sputtered into town, its tank nearly dry. Doc Wilson stepped out of the cab.

"We overpaid for those!" Kumar reminded him.

Rummaging through the truck, Kumar found it empty—save for a large crate of books. All of them were Bibles.

"Apparently," Doc Wilson said with a grim smile, "they expect us to read our way to good health. Through prayer."

"And the ink? The paper? For printing our own books and newspapers?" Kumar pressed.

Wilson, who had seen more suffering than any one man should, didn't answer. Instead, he turned toward the sound of an approaching wagon—three and a half wheels creaking under the weight. The horse pulling it was soaked in sweat. The driver looked worse.

"On back order," Dubois croaked as he collapsed from the buckboard. One of the damaged wheels finally gave way. His coat opened as he hit the ground, and the hood on his head slipped off, revealing a body beaten to a pulp—tarred and feathered.

Wilson and Kumar ran to him as his breath turned into a death rattle.

"All our printing supplies," Dubois managed, "are on back order… till hell freezes over, Comrade Cowboys…" He faded into unconsciousness.

Leona rushed over with Wilson's bag in one hand and her own satchel of earth-grown medicinals in the other.

"Who did this?!" Kumar demanded.

"Someone who, if given the chance," Doc Wilson said grimly, "will do the same to us."

"Or worse," Leona added, as she and Wilson worked in seamless, silent tandem. "Unless I can bring in some redskin Reds to help us out, kinder-than-he-should-be Comrade King Kumar. But you know organizing Indians is as tough as getting Sam Longmore to do a Sundance with fake buffalo horns in his chest—or to even step into a sweat lodge. Or you telling me why you traded your turban in California for a Stetson here. Speaking of which… anyone heard from Sam?"

"I just did," Jake said, stepping in. He held a letter— possibly from the last government mail delivery they'd ever receive. Kumar saw the flicker of fear in Jake's eyes as he read it. A man usually firm in his convictions was suddenly shaken.

As Leona and Wilson fought to bring Dubois back from the edge, Kumar rushed to read over Jake's shoulder. Jake turned away, shielding the letter.

"It was addressed to me!" he barked, cornered and defensive.

"But it concerns us," Leona said, pointing firmly at her chest.

"Come on, son," Father Smith said, placing a strong, steady hand on Jake's trembling shoulder. "Jesus said, 'Thou shalt not lie. Particularly if telling the truth shall benefit another man, or woman—or one conflicted as to who he or she really is.'"

Leona looked up from her work, eyebrow arched. "I don't recall Jesus saying that."

"Well, he did," Smith insisted. Then he winked.

"In your enlightened dreams," Leona whispered to Kumar, recognizing the quote as part of the Gospel according to Father Smith.

Jake, now clutching the letter with trembling hands, considered swallowing it. Smith opened one of the American Bibles they'd received in place of medicine.

"And Jesus also said," he declared, "'He who destroys with his body or closed mind anything that might help his brethren is destroying his chance to enter the kingdom of heaven.'"

Jake paused. "Where did Jesus say that?"

"The Sermon on Mount Gehosiphus," Smith replied without blinking—believing, perhaps, his own fabrication.

Kumar glanced at Jake's doubting face, then to Leona's concern, then to Smith's bluff. For the first time, Kumar wondered if he and his fellow truth-seekers had gone too far with their experiments in benevolent deception.

Before Kumar, Leona, or Smith could get an answer from their respective deities about what to do next, the answer came instead—from a mortal on Earth.

"The Sermon on Mount Gehosiphus. I remember it well," said Doc Wilson, sounding every bit the all-knowing scholar, even as his hands—wiser than his head—stitched Dubois's wounds with expert care.

"Where our Lord said… 'A man who tells less than the truth is less than a man,'" continued the former God-loving Christian, now an atheist pagan after witnessing too many of the 'Good Heavenly Father's' children die ugly, premature deaths. He recited the words as if reading them from a divine cloud drifting above. "At the temple. In the workplace. And…"

"…in the bedchamber of the woman he loves," Father Smith interjected, his voice in divinely timed harmony. "In the original translation, that is," he added.

Jake scratched his head—hair finally grown in—and pulled back his lips into a thoughtful half-smile. "Well, Father, Doc, if you say so," he muttered. He handed over a letter from their mutual boss, Sam—a man who was, for different reasons, a friend to each of them. Kumar read it, his expression shifting to concern, then shock.

"Yer better at book-learnin' in them old languages, Padre Smith," Jake slurred, eyes cast down, more defeated than Kumar had ever seen him, in public or private. "While I'm, I suppose… just a cowboy who, ya know…"

"Is, thankfully for the moment, functionally illiterate?" Leona whispered to Smith.

Smith gave a gentle nod, easing her concern.

"…Yeah… I'm an American-born and -bred cowboy," Jake continued, kicking at the dirt with his boots as though kicking himself. "Who…"

"…'Can accept this offer from Sergeant Sam—now Captain Longmore—to join the other side in this war. If you want to. Or need to,'" Kumar read aloud from the letter addressed solely to Jake—and to Buddy, if Jake chose to share it. "'Top-grade pay. Security for you and any future family you'll have. And amnesty for any criminal actions you committed—or didn't commit.'" He handed the letter back.

"The easy and smart thing ain't always the right thing. And the hardest thing is sometimes the rightest thing," Jake said, recalling both his Pa's voice and Sam's teachings. "Jesus musta said that, didn't He?" he asked Smith.

"And He lived it too," Smith replied, from the depths of a heart that had bent the truth more than once—but still longed to live it.

"As will I," Jake declared, his gaze fixed on past and future at once. With that, he tore open the contract offered by Sam. It was a bold, reckless, and—at least for Jake—potentially destructive decision. But it was made.

At that exact moment, a voice rose from the grave—no less miraculous than Lazarus praising Jesus after being raised from the dead.

"What happened?" Dubois said, waking from the cocktail of herbal and factory-made anesthetics that had knocked him out long enough for Doc Wilson to stitch him together. "Where am I?" asked the tireless labor organizer, who had always worked harder than any man beneath or above him. It was a question Kumar found himself silently asking, too.

"In the middle of an epidemic," came a high-pitched voice—scared and pure all at once. "According to the signs outside town," Elsa Steiner continued as she hopped down from her horse-drawn, one-axle cart. The 10-year-old, already 90 at heart, was determined to grow up into far more than just another good-hearted, baby-making woman. She held up one of the official signs she'd pulled from the outskirts of town. "'Plague. Quarantined. Entry Forbidden. By Order of the Governor,'" she read aloud.

"Don't believe everything you read, Elsa," Doc Wilson told the frightened girl, whose mother—still in the cart—let out a dry, scratchy cough.

"But believe in what you write," Kumar said, something larger than himself stirring inside. Inspired, he grabbed a paintbrush from outside the general store and scrawled his answer across the sign.

"I'm a better talker than a writer," he explained, as he worked.

"But in the meantime…" Leona added.

"…This loses NOTHING in translation," she finished with a smile, reading aloud: "FAKE plague. Entry WELCOMED. By order of 'THE PEOPLE,' WHICH IS YOU AND US."

Kumar grabbed the altered sign and began painting the same message on the rest still stacked in the cart. Once the paint dried, he loaded them onto a travois, mounted his lightly harnessed horse, Arjun, and rode toward town from the East.

When he reached Blue Water's official boundary—the place where most comings and goings had occurred for generations—he hammered the signs into the hard, unyielding earth, nearly breaking his fist from the force he used to make them stick.

A cold wind swept across the back of his sweat-drenched neck. It blew down from the North, heading straight for the warm clouds rising from the South. He could smell the onset of a dry snowfall. He felt it, too—in the soles of his feet and the pit of his gut, just beneath his loaded revolver belt.

The earth murmured. Something was coming. Something that would soon demand those bullets be used for more than the head of a dying cow, the skull of a crippled horse, or the chest of a bear-eaten man—or woman.

Kumar's ears twitched before his eyes confirmed the sound. Three green military trucks appeared on the far end of the valley to the East. Concealed by brush along the riverbank, he raised binoculars from his saddlebag.

He saw soldiers—armed, uniformed, organized—leaping from the lead vehicle. From the two others, men in striped uniforms and chains were forced out. Kumar noted the half-shaven heads, the chains, the military caps. All were assembling a fence stretching as far as the eye could see. Other official-looking vehicles flanked them. More armed men emerged. Fences went up—strong enough to stop cattle, horses, or any civilian vehicle Kumar knew of.

A high-ranking American officer trotted along the fence line, long rifle strapped to his back, pointing with his swagger stick where mines and bear traps were to be planted. Kumar recognized both the horse and its rider.

"Yeah… old friends," Kumar said grimly to Arjun. "Sergeant Sam—now Captain Longmore—reunited with his favorite horse, Chief."

He turned Arjun around. "Suppose we need to get into town. Get more paint. More signs."

He mounted, resolved. "And painters," he added. "People with better penmanship than me, more colorful in their verbiage, and—"

His thought was cut short by a bullet slamming into the dirt inches in front of Arjun's feet. The startled horse spun left in panic. Two more shots rang out. Whether they hit the ground, horseflesh, or human skin remained to be seen. By grace or grit, Kumar held on—gripping Arjun's flanks and the reins, holding steady against the fear.

When he'd regained control, he looked up to find the shooter. A lone sharpshooter stood high above. The face was obscured by the brim of a hat—perhaps Sam Longmore, perhaps someone else.

Another shot. This one struck one of Kumar's signs, joining two earlier bullet holes—each one precisely obliterating his handwritten message.

The sharpshooter raised the rifle again.

Kumar, fearing the next round would be for Arjun, waved a casual, friendly "see ya later," and rode away.

"Yes, Arjun," he said, voice low but resolute. "We need people who can paint, shoot, and bullshit better than I ever could."

CHAPTER 13

The next morning, under cover of a thankfully foggy night, Kumar returned to 'the front'. This time, he was clad in the turban his grandfather had bequeathed to him, along with his final letter. Maybe it possessed magical powers, or maybe it didn't. He would soon find out, as would the artistically gifted citizens—sign painters armed with paintbrushes, and those who, rightly or wrongly, were more skilled at ejecting lead from steel barrels or flaming arrows from bows. They all held positions deep in the bush, visible from above but concealed from the fence builders and mine planters across the valley.

Among the Paleface defenders, replacing government signs with custom-made messages welcoming brave, curious, or homeless souls to Blue River, were Jake, Buddy, and the still-standing but deeply injured Dubois. Their orders were clear: fire warning shots near enemy combatants' feet and unleash upon any mechanized metal beasts. The sign painters, a mix of Red, White, and Black-skinned Rembrandts in the making, were instructed to express their thoughts and feelings on their canvases. One artist, armed with a machine gun for protection against fence-building

Uniformed Palefaces, carried with him a sense of humor and a unique vitality that Kumar found most concerning, especially when directed at a special someone through his artwork.

"You sure about this treaty with the Palefaces?" Chief Russell asked Leona, as she aimed a machine gun towards fence builders on the distant hills, while he focused on his sign with brush strokes flowing like a musical river from his hand. Kumar overheard the exchange with his keen sense of hearing, confirmed by his exceptional lip-reading skills.

"As sure as I am that any marriage with you would've been hell for both of us," Leona replied, using the machine gun to dissuade six fence builders from their task. The gun had been acquired from bootleggers Chief Russell had unintentionally scalped—palefaces from Chicago who sought profit by converting his traditional dry reserve into a drunk tank. "Yeah, any marriage with you would've been bad medicine for both of us," Leona reiterated, recalling the good times amidst the bad.

"Maybe," Chief Russell acknowledged, torn between feelings about the unfulfilled dream of a 'match made in The Happy Hunting Grounds' with Leona. "But I'm a more witty artist than your Comrade Mayor," he continued, a rival who outmatched Kumar in looks, strength, financial stability, charm, and genetics. "We all take liberation too seriously," Russell quipped, revealing his sign to Leona, eliciting a carefree laughter that Kumar had rarely witnessed from her, especially not with him or anyone else.

"A step towards changing your mind and opening that closed heart," Russell remarked with a self-assured smile.

"Yes... a big step," Leona replied, her laughter subsiding as she admired Russell's Herculean physique while he hammered the sign into the ground. The writing, in three languages including what appeared to be Russian and two Native tongues, was adorned with intricate designs featuring local wildlife, asserting their presence in Blue River.

"A private joke between them, no doubt," Kumar heard a high-pitched voice comment behind him. "An invitation to others to embrace the growth and bliss of your social experiment."

"Our experiment, Elsa," Kumar responded to the eleven-year-old literary prodigy of Blue River, wise beyond her years. He glanced at her art, dressed in a cowboy ensemble that fit her surprisingly well but was mismatched with her still-long hair, despite her persistent requests for an Amelia Earhart haircut. "Enough soldiers up there?" she queried, fearless.

"Enough," Kumar affirmed.

"And we're changing signs that nobody will read because?" Elsa pressed, assertive yet respectful. "Don't tell me I'll understand when I'm older, like everyone else."

Kumar pondered his response to the girl who chose risking her life in the hills over reading about history safely in a library. "This land belongs to the people," Kumar asserted, feeling connected to his Sikh revolutionary grandfather's spirit and wisdom. "Right now, we are the people. If we create welcoming signs like..."

"... This one?" Elsa interrupted, seeking Kumar's approval. His smile of pride reflected his surrogate goddaughter's talent, though he still focused on areas for improvement, a critical eye tempered by paternal pride. But before he could delve into a critique, laughter erupted again—Leona's laughter. Kumar glanced her way.

"Is something wrong?" Elsa asked, sensing Kumar's displeasure.

"No, everything's great with what you've done," Kumar assured her truthfully.

"And with what he's done?" Elsa persisted, noticing Chief Russell's completion of another sign that brought even more laughter from Leona, culminating in a loving embrace.

"Leona seems happy," Elsa observed.

"Yeah... I know," Kumar admitted reluctantly, his fist tightening with an emotion he struggled to contain.

"Aren't we supposed to be happy for others when they're happy?" Elsa queried, teacher-like in her insight. Kumar saw concern lines trying to form on her angelic face, destined to always be alone, even if loved. "Isn't love enjoying others' joy vicariously?"

"Yeah… theoretically," Kumar admitted. "But when it comes to happiness, bliss, and—at least as far as I've stumbled into it—the wisdom to—"

A thunderous rumble interrupted his thoughts. Vehicles moved in louder and heavier from the other side of the valley. Kumar raised his binoculars and spotted three supervising soldiers emerging from armored trucks, followed by a ragged line of men. These workers had clearly lost a third of their body weight but not the right to choose their own clothing—or rags, rather. The 'hobo' detail began fastening thick, vicious strands of barbed wire to the posts already threaded with thin, warning lines.

"Who are those people?" Elsa asked.

"Un-evolved souls in uniforms with guns," Kumar replied, eyeing the clean-shaven soldiers dressed in sharply tailored attire that gave their frail shoulders the illusion of strength—like figures from a George Washington portrait. "And wage slaves who don't know that selling out to feed their families can destroy a thousand others," he added, referring to the civilians doing the manual labor.

"What bad things?" Elsa pressed.

Kumar opened his mouth to answer but stopped himself. To answer truthfully would mean revealing far more than he was ready to.

"So," Elsa shot back, folding her small arms across a chest just beginning to bloom into womanhood, "you're not going to tell me because I'm a girl and can't handle it?!"

"No," Kumar replied, still avoiding her eyes. He knew she could see straight through him. "Because you… well…"

"Because well what?!" she demanded, stepping in front of him, forcing eye contact.

Before Kumar could respond, a harsh, metallic clank shattered the conversation. Elsa turned, startled. The noise sounded like bones being crushed in hell. In a heartbeat, she wrapped her thin arms around Kumar's chest—solid and unmoving to her, a child seeking the safety of a stone wall.

A beast of metal, shaped like a dragon, was pushing through the valley. The bulldozer tore the earth apart without mercy, creating a grotesque wall of dirt and carving trenches on both sides. Jagged wire and leg traps were tossed into these "moats," meant to maim anyone who dared cross— friend or foe.

Prisoners in striped suits hauled heavy cannons into place, chains clinking around their ankles. Others pounded stakes into the ground with bare, bleeding hands. A foreman on horseback barked orders and lashed stragglers with a whip.

"This is a work detail!" he screamed. "So work, you miserable, lazy pieces of shit! Work, you hobos, you were bitching about being out of work—now work!"

"And who are… or were… those men in the chains?" Elsa asked, loosening her grip on Kumar and focusing on the suffering of strangers over the comfort of herself.

Kumar raised his rifle, pressing the stock to his shoulder and taking aim. "Men who are about to take the day off," he said grimly.

"And the rest of the week," Leona added, appearing at Kumar's side with her bow and arrow. She grabbed the lighter from his breast pocket—completely ignoring the chest beneath it—and prepared to ignite the twine-wrapped, oil-soaked arrow tip.

"Or the month," Chief Russell chimed in, hauling over a portable machine gun. Ammo belts draped across his broad shoulders, each weighing nearly half as much as he did.

"Or the mother-fucking year!" Elsa declared, pulling a slingshot from beneath her oversized shirttail.

"Hey!" Chief Russell shouted, incredulous. "Where did you learn that kind of language?"

"My Pa," Elsa shot back as she loaded one of Leona's rock-hard fireballs into her slingshot, aiming it at the Foreman above. Then, suddenly, she seemed to see something—something in the faces of the oppressed souls in chains, or perhaps in the eyes of the ignorant ones who kept them in bondage. Her beet-red face, hot with fury, began to be washed over by tears of grief. But it was grief that demanded to be nullified—by action.

"Her father was a labor organizer who got tossed in jail," Kumar quietly explained to Russell. "Tortured by the cops, starved in solitary, poisoned the day before the Labor Union finally got him released to be sent home…"

"...In a fucking box!" Elsa yelled, apparently hearing Kumar despite the distance. "Dead. Just like those fucking goons and scabs on top of us are going to be."

She stood up from her previously hidden position, placing herself squarely in the line of sight—and fire—of the foreman and the heavily armed soldiers "supervising" the chain gang and the so-called 'free' laborers. "A whole lot of people are going to be dead after today," she growled, the master slingshot shooter of Blue River and all its surrounding counties, her voice laced with grit and defiance.

"But not you," Leona interjected with a caring smile and warm, protective eyes, gently attempting to pry the slingshot from Elsa's hands.

Leona edged one hand toward the weapon and the other to the back of Elsa's shirt, then her long mane of braided hair, pulling her down and out of sight from the well-positioned troops. "The revolution needs you to run—back home," she whispered urgently, with as much logic and tenderness as she could muster.

Elsa responded to Leona's wisdom with the same fierce resistance Leona herself had once given when others tried to protect her under the guise of keeping her small and safe.

Kumar hadn't known Elsa's skills with fists, feet, and teeth were so advanced. Apparently, neither had Leona. But Leona never backed down from a fight—and she wasn't about to now.

"You have to go home, Elsa!" Kumar shouted as the two girls wrestled. He tried to push between them. "To warn everybody else about what might happen, okay? To protect your mother… and every other mother… and—"

His sentence was cut short as he caught blows from both girls, tumbling backward into a tree beside Russell.

"That speech is supposed to work," he muttered through a mouth full of pain, though it was reconnecting to his brain.

"You forgot to put it in future tense, brown-skinned paleface," Chief Russell replied, unpredictable as ever.

Russell reached into Kumar's pocket, pulled out a joint and a pen. He tossed the joint, stamping it into the dirt with the fury of a raging bull. Then he gently handed the pen to Elsa, who was mid-swing at Leona's belly with her tiny but lethal fist.

"Take this weapon," he said to the young literary prodigy, holding out the pen. "State-of-the-art. Doesn't even need to be dipped in ink every third line."

Elsa paused, startled, and looked up at the pen. That hesitation gave Leona a chance to escape what surely would have been a stomach-crushing blow—one that might have ended her day as a fighter… and her future as a mother.

Russell gently placed the writing instrument into Elsa's tender, already bruised hand.

"You can fight these shitheads with a stone-age slingshot and be killed and forgotten," he said, his voice low and steady. "Or use this pen to write down what's about to happen here. Exactly as it happens. For this generation… and the ones to come."

"The pen is mightier than the sword," Kumar added, feeling woefully inadequate for not having his own original line.

"Yeah—especially when you jab the sharp end into your enemy's eye. Or heart," Leona grunted, pushing herself upright on sore, battered feet.

"The world needs your mind and your voice, Elsa," Russell said, now less a Chief and more a professor. "And one day, your heart. When you're older."

Then, switching to German, he added:

"Like your great-grandfather who fought against kings and capitalist tyrants in 1848. And when he came here—to fight the pro-slavers in grey, and after that, the white-hooded Klansmen. Verstehen Sie?"

"Ja. Ich verstehe," Elsa replied, her accent flavored with Texas German passed down through generations.

She took the pen, mounted her horse, and rode toward town.

Leona hugged Russell in gratitude. The gesture evolved into a kiss—his lips moving gently across her bruises, then finding hers.

"Eh… Leona," Kumar began, the words bubbling up from his gut. The kiss continued. Their bodies and souls fell into one another, sharing a bliss that had spanned this life—and perhaps others.

"I didn't know Chief Russell… hmm… spoke German. And was good with Elsa. And…"

Having had his fill of watching other people fall in love, and aware that trumpets might call them all to battle at any moment, Kumar dared to break the moment. He tapped their shoulders. Their eyes remained closed. Leona held up five fingers in his direction.

"Sure. Five seconds. Indian time," Kumar muttered.

Her answer: five fingers, flashed three times.

"So…" Kumar waited impatiently while the woman he wanted and the man he respected fell deeper into one another. To distract himself, he looked through his binoculars at the other side of the valley. He spotted bare-handed prisoners constructing a fence of flesh-slicing barbed wire.

One face froze him.

"What the fuck… Sheriff? Colonel? Sergeant—now Inmate—Johnston?" he whispered.

Leona and Russell broke their kiss. Kumar passed Russell the binoculars with reverence. Leona snatched them instead.

"I thought Johnston was the first asshole we were supposed to scalp!" she spat, raising them to her eyes.

"Someone else may have beat you to it," Kumar said, noting Johnston's half-shaved head—bare of even stubble, like the rest of the prisoners.

"We take him alive," Kumar said, lifting his rifle.

"So I can scalp the rest of his head," Leona growled.

"Depends what's in that head," Russell added calmly.

"And what he plans to do with it," Kumar replied, picking up the slingshot Elsa had left behind. "You two—or anyone else got anything stronger than this Goliath slayer?" he asked, stuffing branches into his coat and turban. "Something that can take out the vehicles—the bulldozer, and any tanks. No people, not yet."

He began crawling up the hill, camouflaged as a walking tree. From the top, he spotted another wave of soldiers moving in.

"And when they fire at us again?" Leona asked.

The walking tree paused. "This revolution has two agendas," Kumar said. "One: Above all, do no harm—not intentionally, anyway. Two: Make the biggest, motherfucking, shit-blasting impact possible."

"Being a doctor who heals the world, and a warrior who liberates it," Russell mused, scratching his chin. "Like diving into a pool of shit and trying not to get wet or stink."

"Just do it!" Kumar shouted back, just as a gust of wind shoved a mouthful of branches down his throat. "On the count of—" Another burst of leaves filled his mouth. He reached into his pocket for his grandfather's watch.

Empty.

"Anyone HERE have a watch?" he shouted, spitting out twigs.

"Used to…" Russell replied.

"Work according to the clock, and you get enslaved by it," Leona added.

"Then fire away when the shadow of those rocks hits the river," Kumar said, trying to devise the best natural sundial available. But then he saw another problem. "Or if the clouds move in… again," he added, flashing on an idea that was somehow more practical and witty than anything Chief Russell or any of his legendary comic-warrior superhero ancestors had ever come up with. "Say 'Kumar is a misunderstood genius' one hundred times."

"Positive self-talk he does to himself," Leona explained to Russell, "which never works."

"Repeating is believing," Kumar said directly—perhaps too directly—to Leona, before slithering off.

"I fucking well hope so," Kumar heard Leona mutter behind him.

"So do I," Russell added.

Kumar worked his way into the brush behind the prisoners, close enough to the mounted Foreman to smell the whiskey on his breath. Along the way, he realized he'd put his grandfather's pocket watch in the other pocket.

"You lazy idiots!" the Foreman shouted at the inmates between lashes of his whip, most of which struck their targets. "You're working to protect America. My America. Your family's America. The America that birthed your father's shame. Your—"

Kumar grabbed the business end of the whip just as the Foreman pulled back to strike again—this time at the slowest and oldest prisoner, who, ironically, turned out to be Johnston. A sharp yank disarmed the Foreman. A rock launched from Elsa's slingshot slammed into the horse's flank, throwing the Foreman to the ground. A cloth soaked in chloroform from Kumar's medical kit silenced him into unconsciousness. Kumar gagged him just in case, then bound his wrists and ankles with rope.

He snatched the key ring from the Foreman and unlocked the first prisoner on the chain gang, motioning urgently for each freed man to unshackle the next. The stunned prisoners obeyed.

Kumar checked the time—his watch had stopped. With a sigh, he tucked it back into his pocket, hoping someone in town might be able to fix it... if he ever made it back there alive.

"In twenty 'Kumar Patel is a misunderstood genius' incantations," he said, donning the Foreman's hat and coat and mounting the horse, "you run for your still-valuable lives."

He turned, doing his best impression of the gagged Foreman:

"You miserable, despicable pieces of shit!"

"Not anymore," Kumar heard Johnston say, now unshackled and passing the key to the next man—a task he took on with both vigor and gratitude.

Across the valley, Leona and Russell took position on high ground, hidden but with a clear view of the approaching troops. Russell, as was his habit since fighting in the War to End All Wars as an underage soldier, marked a line in the sand for each enemy he saw.

Joining them, ducking low, was Buddy Emerson—second fiddle to any leader, even one who couldn't play the violin.

"Buddy Emerson is a misunderstood genius," Leona said loudly enough for the gun-toting cowboy—who had only just managed to grow a mustache this year—to hear.

Next to arrive, limping and still injured, was Dubois, rifle slung in his good arm.

"Emerson Dubois is an underrated hero," Leona declared, adding another chant to the countdown.

Then came Jake.

"Jake Hanson is still a misogynist, racist asshole," Leona stated, right on beat.

Jake responded with a long, slow middle finger from his left hand, the right one aiming his Winchester toward their shared enemy. Leona clenched her fist, ready to return the salute, but Russell gently lowered her wrist.

He pointed to the sand. Ninety enemy marks. Only twelve Blue River fighters.

As the 'so-and-so is a so-and-so' chants approached ninety-nine, Russell counted down silently on his fingers.

Meanwhile, Kumar—dressed as the Foreman—herded the disguised chain gang forward toward a well-armed battalion. Three more trucks rolled in from the east, carrying ammunition, cannons, machine guns, building materials, and fresh soldiers.

"And in… five, four, three, two…" Kumar whispered to the now-free men masquerading as prisoners.

Russell and the others opened fire. Most of the soldiers ducked for cover, surprised. Some of the former prisoners, led by Johnston, charged, seizing weapons from the startled troops. Others fled down the hill, unarmed. A few, perhaps too broken to run, re-shackled themselves and refused the rifles tossed to them by Johnston.

Johnston led his band of rebels past a bulldozer. Once clear, a flaming arrow hit its metal flank. It burst into flame, its mechanical guts raining down like shrapnel.

Five soldiers—ordered by what appeared to be a colonel—rushed toward the ammo truck. Machine gun fire from Russell's team stopped them cold. Another flaming arrow from Leona struck the truck, setting off a deafening explosion that returned the ammunition and guns to their chemical components.

Most of the enlisted men turned tail and ran eastward into the woods, leaving behind boots, hats, and probably a generous amount of piss in their trousers. The rest stood their ground, firing back at Kumar's "Communist Anarchists" and "redskin renegades" with intense, chaotic rage.

As for the civilian laborers, some of them ran towards Kumar's side of the line, the rest into the woods. The few soldiers who still held the line as more gunfire from the Comrade side of the valley received bullets in front of their feet and into their hats every time they tried to get up.

Before heading back to the other side of the valley, a mounted Kumar shed the Forman's coat and hat and gazed with delight at the display. No one was killed or wounded. But there was one brave soldier who seemed to want to have blood spilled on the ground, from both sides.

"Get back here!" Captain Sam Longmore yelled to the wave of conscripted soldiers and hired civilians retreating back into the woods, hightailing it for somewhere safe. "Like Sergeant Jones here!" he blasted at the cowards, referring to the man still next to him on his side of the 'trench'. "And Private Newman, who.." Sam looked at the two men, as did Kumar from his location. Indeed, those two heroes stayed at their posts because they couldn't move. Both shook like leaves, terror in their catatonic faces. It was the first time Kumar had seen shell shock, but certainly not so for Sam, the veteran of the War to End All Wars. "Colonel Daniels!" Sam yelled out to his apparently commanding officer, safely in an armored car behind him. "We have orders to hold our ground! Call for reinforcements."

"Not today, Captain," Daniels screamed back, having put down a portable radio. "New orders. We're pulling back. And you ARE coming with us!" With that, Daniels' relatively sheltered driver finally got the engine going. "That means NOW, Captain!"

Kumar took a moment to look at Sam as he decided what to do. Sam gazed back at his former surrogate son to whom he wished to pass on his Life Torch, but this time as an enemy. One that Cowboy Sam and now Captain Longmore hated, feared, and pitied. Kumar returned the same feelings, then rode down the hill, just in time for shots from a rifle he recognized all too well to be fired at Sam. It forced him out of the trench and into the armored vehicle with Daniels, which disappeared into the Eastern horizon, ten times quicker than it arrived.

"There ya go…Just made my old boss dance to my tune…" Kumar heard Jake say upon his arrival back on the Comrade side of the line, after Jake had emptied the last of his supply of bullets from his Winchester at Sam's feet.

"So, you did, Jake…So you did," Leona said with pride.

"Good shooting," Kumar said to the detachment of Comrade shooters. "No one killed anyone. Including me."

"Not yet," Leona warned.

"Thankfully," Russell noted, after which he addressed Kumar with a name the EAST Indian didn't recognize with a courtly bow and poker face.

"What did he call me?" Kumar asked Leona.

"Your new AMERICAN Indian name," she said proudly.

"Which means?" Kumar inquired.

"Loosely translated," she said with regret through a mouth unaccustomed to the taste of eating crow. "Kumar Patel is a misunderstood genius and revolutionary visionary."

"Which me like," Kumar replied with a proud shit eating grin.

"Who will be given a warrior's burial sooner than he planned for?" Russell said with admiration and regret. With that, the Chief motioned for his Indian buds to follow his departure, some of whom were wounded.

"Where are they going?" Kumar inquired of Leona.

"Somewhere I have to go too, for now...temporarily," her reply with lowered eyes, which seemed to hold more secrets than usual. Made even more secretive by the way she hugged Kumar, with the deepest of affections. Without a word said, she joined Russell and the exodus of every American Indian who had joined in the East Indian's 'all races included' crusade.

"What do they know that I don't?" Kumar inquired of Jake.

"And we don't," Kumar's former rival and now, perhaps, best bud replied. "What did we do wrong?" Jake asked Kumar, fearing that within victory there was defeat.

"We woke up a sleeping giant," Kumar said with remorse and pride. "Or worse...showed him what he really is. But...Jesus said...Blessed be the peacemakers."

"For they shall die, as I recall?" Jake countered.

"Not without transforming the world, and themselves," Kumar said as he mounted his own horse for the solemn ride back home, inviting Jake to do the same. "And entering the kingdom of heaven...where..."

"…Horses never get tired and always do what you want them to 'cause they want to do it also, and never give you any back talk about it?" Jake asked and claimed.

"You bet," Kumar assured Jake, trying his best to believe in that white lie.

"And buckle bunny babes laugh at all of my jokes, even the bad ones?" Jake asked his new friend, and perhaps mentor.

"Sure thing," Kumar replied, testing out the theory that if you act like a leader who knows what they are doing, you will become one.

"And no one is gonna try ta trick me into thinking that what's written on a page is what they want me ta believe is there?" Jake gently pressed.

"Absolutely…hmmm… Yes," Kumar replied, knowing that one of the weapons he would not have at his disposal for the battles ahead was to be a convincing liar. An armament which, unfortunately, his adversaries were experts at.

CHAPTER 14

Wentworth always trusted that the newspapers—especially those he paid good money to co-own—would tell him what he wanted to hear. What he didn't bargain for was having them present, in unmistakable black-and-white print with no room for gray, exactly what he needed to hear.

Still, he read on—aloud—from the New York Herald Gazette, seated behind his desk in what was still his eagle's nest atop a towering skyscraper, overlooking the two-legged human field mice scurrying below.

"Jackson County, from its capital of Blue River, Colorado, declared independence yet again today—as a self-reliant community. Taking what it needs from Mother Nature and serving all of Mama N's children's needs—and wants—with more children of all ages arriving every day, and now, every night. Running through or going around the blockade that remains in place. Some with no worldly possessions. Seeking survival…"

Wentworth paused, recalling a prior issue of the same paper that ran a personal interest story on the dirt-poor, empty-bellied, and barely clothed Okie migrants who risked imprisonment or death just to become citizens of a new country—rather than remain bottom feeders in the one they were born into.

"Some gave up their worldly possessions, seeking a new salvation… a new covenant with the Almighty."

Wentworth read the words with escalating, though still controlled, rage. He remembered the sermon he'd attended at St. Patrick's Cathedral—strictly for the purpose of currying favor with Joseph Kennedy, then the most successful of Boston's Irish nouveau riche mobsters. A young padre had filled in for the usual priest that day, telling the congregation how seminarians and nuns had quietly looted the drug supply rooms of five high-end hospitals and two army bases en route to Denver. Then, under moonlight and under cover of captured U.S. Army cannons—retrofitted to fire boluses of foul, fog-producing manure—they ran through the blockade.

"And some came because they wanted to make history rather than comfortably write about and interpret it."

Wentworth gritted his teeth as he read. The mogul who had risen from riches to even greater riches thought now of his sister's summa cum laude Harvard Law graduate boyfriend, and his double-Ph.D. girlfriend in English and Political Science. They had stolen a car and slipped through the blockade—bringing with them books they had bought, borrowed, or outright stolen. They were now Deans at the newly established university in Blue River. A town that, prior to the "revolution," had little more than a two-room schoolhouse for children under twelve, and a high school barely equipped to serve a handful of teens and knowledge-hungry adults.

"Miraculously, no one on either side of the blockade has been killed in the skirmishes between the haves and the former have-nots—who have become haves, because they share what they have, or what they can get. But what has been killed is—"

Wentworth slammed the paper onto his desk. He inhaled deeply through his oversized nostrils, feeling a knot form in his giant-sized gut. He waited for his overworked heart to slow, pounding less fiercely in his chest, and finally spoke to his guest.

"What has been killed," he said, "is journalistic integrity. This 'story'—fact or fiction, as we both know and should realize—is being picked up by established newspapers, run by established men, in established cities. And it was written by..." He took another breath, more laborious than the last. "Written by a ten-year-old girl! Elsa Steiner, she calls herself. And her propaganda-spinning coaches."

"Who are more resilient than I thought," said Sam Longmore, calmly smoking a cigar.

"But it's temporary."

"How temporary, Captain—and if our other plan doesn't work, Private or Inmate Longmore?" Wentworth pressed, leaning back in his chair. As always, composure returned when his back was against the wall.

"Our plan being…?" Longmore asked, puzzled now.

Knowing the value—and pleasure—of keeping his business partners and potential rivals confounded about his true thoughts and intentions, Wentworth pulled a manila folder from the left drawer of his usually locked desk. He handed it to Sam, who set down his cigar and read the contents with a mix of admiration, concern, and curiosity.

"Some supplemental plans," Wentworth said casually, "to what we already discussed."

He lit his own cigar, blowing perfect smoke rings into the air and toward Longmore's furrowed brow.

"Plans which you will not discuss with anyone else. Because we are counting on two things that are always true in any game between competitors—regardless of ideology."

"That absolute power corrupts—absolutely," Sam said, conceding the point. "True enough. As I… we… look in the mirror, sir."

His eyes wandered, drawn—just as Wentworth intended—to the mirror behind the mogul's desk. A clever trap to distract, or disarm, the most self-absorbed of his 'partners.' Longmore's stare lingered. Something in his reflection seemed to trouble him… and something else seemed to embolden him.

"And," Wentworth continued smoothly, "that nature never gives you a problem without a solution."

"In this case…" Sam began.

"Something that can be done—legally," Longmore finished, the assertion steadier now. He'd read the plans, seen the path, and glimpsed the contours of his own evolving—or perhaps devolving—soul as one of its architects.

"And something we must do, any way you have to, Sam," Wentworth said, using Longmore's first name for the first time. It carried weight. A fellow Christian's summons in service of a Capitalist Christian country. "Because, well… you, me, and Him above us all know why."

CHAPTER 15

There was one thing that Mother Nature always provided Jackson County and Blue River, and that was water through an always flowing stream of that necessity for all life for which the town got its name. The spring thaw came early, releasing a torrent of water flowing down from the still snow-covered hills into the river which spoke to anyone who dared, or wanted, to listen to it. But as for this year, that water was being diverted elsewhere by dam builders. This time it was not an army of deforesting beavers moving sticks from point A to B, but two legged human varmints armed with weapons far more deadly than sharp teeth or hard flapping tails. The company of Army, Police and civil engineers building the dam very legally just outside the limits of Jackson County worked like an armada of workaholic, supercharged beavers. It turned the river flowing through Jackson County from an eight of a mile wide, five story deep rhythmically flowing body of clear aqua into a slowly moving sludge of mud which got shallower and narrower with each layer of the concrete, lumber and steel enforced dam laid into the all too easily penetrated earth. At the rate they were building, it would a matter of days until the river that flowed even in the driest of seasons would become a valley of dried mud littered with dead skeletons from dehydrated animals and people.

With a parched throat, mounted on top of a still well-watered Arjun, Kumar beheld with his terrified eyes and painful ears the wonders of modern technology diverting a river which, when it wanted to, decided to flood over its banks in the constant battle between the principalities of water and earth.

"He who has the biggest guns and is prepared to USE them controls the law," Leona commented atop her appaloosa stallion, who, for her anyway, was as obedient as any well broke gelding.

"He who controls the law controls the river," Chief Russell added, seated very comfortably on a nearly full blood Arab mare who, because she was of the highest thinking breed of horse, was the least popular in most areas of the state.

"And he who controls the river controls..." Leona appended.

"......All of the people and animals it   feeds," Kumar barked back.

"Or fed," Leona informed him, this time holding back most of her 'I could have told ya so if you asked' eye-roll. "Which means that..."

"...You two are going back to the still water fed Rez, to save what's left of your people," Kumar replied.

"Because White Democratic Socialists still don't want to include Red Indians into your Revolution," Leona informed him in a hard-hitting soft tone.

"Which is NOT MY fucking fault!" Kumar shouted back, trying to believe that claim. "I begged, asked and pleaded with them to do the right thing by your people."

"But you didn't MAKE them do the effective thing for my people! While…ahhh…

you still refer to MY people as your FAVORITE people or YOU people, Comrade Philosopher Coordinator Kumar!"

"Because you refer to my people as your people!" Kumar countered, after which he pinched a fold of loose, prematurely for the season dark brown skin on his forearm. "You see this skin on me! Think it's easy being my kind of brown in a white world?"

"And you think it's easy being directed by a revolutionary who values philosophical

wisdom over force? And power? Who tells your people and my people that we're fighting against a powerful enemy?" Russell offered in that soft tone of his which made you scared of what would happen if you ever heard it raised.

"Power corrupts, absolutely," Kumar related.

"But power is sometimes necessary," she calmly said to Kumar, extending her palm out to his shaking arm. "Like…"

Leona's attempt to alleviate Kumar's fear gave way to dealing with her own visceral pain. Her palm went instantly to her belly. Kumar noted that it was bigger than usual. Out of her mouth came a bolus of vomit, most of which hit the ground rather than the tip of Kumar's boot.

"Yes, necessities," Kumar admitted. "Like you raising that Red-skinned baby of yours

with his own people…I know. Which is…Okay. Really," he continued, pushing his mind into believing what he knew was right in his soul.

"And you, doing whatever you need to, so you can force your people into doing the

Right thing…Instead of inviting them to…" said the Chief who was no doubt the father of the Lakota female Einstein's baby.

Such convinced Leona to contemplate something deep behind her averted contemplative face. She said something in Lakota, then prodded her horse to go back to her new home in the Rez. It lay North of the borders of Jackson County. Russell followed.

"OK, don't tell me what that Lakota credo means!" Kumar yelled out as mother, father and soon to be born into maybe a better or maybe a worse world disappeared into the distance. "I can ask someone else to translate it. I have a smart mind. A powerful mind that…:"

Frustrated, Kumar reached for his reserve friend and crutch. It had been weeks since he smoked a joint, as he was saving imbibing the weed that allowed him escape from the world as it is (and the one he was trying to create) for emergencies only. But just as he brought his lighter to tip of the wackie tobaccie cigarillo, he was presented with a clear glass vial of white powder by a man on horseback whose presence he least expected.

"You can be more powerful, and effective, and clever with this," ex-sheriff, ex colonel, ex-prisoner and now Comrade Johnston said regarding the magic power as he stroked his fingers through his finally fully grown-in symmetrical head of hair. "It was recommended to me by a convicted doc in prison who turned my soul around. And by Doc Wilson to everyone here, just before he left two days ago to recruit more counties and doctors to join us."

"And Doc Wilson recommends this to himself?" Kumar said as he opened up the vial for a test smell.

"When he has to work around the clock to put together what disease and trauma

tore apart," Johnston assured Kumar, as a Comrade in Common Cause rather than a Capitalist snake oil salesman.

Kumar dipped his finger into the vial, then moved it towards his mouth. Johnston placed his hand between Kumar's shaking phalanges, and was hungry for anything that would work oral cavity.

"No…like this," Johnston said, taking three pinches of the white powder with his shooting hand. He placed on his, then snorted all of the white powder up his nose with the voracity that a hungry dog licks a plate coated with beef gravy and giblets.

Johnston's face which had been a minute ago that of an old man tired of living took on a glow of a young one who was eager to embrace three new lifetimes and ten times that number of adventures in each of them. Such looked inviting enough to Kumar.

A strange sensation hit Kumar's nostrils, then head as he snorted in the white powder, after which his nose decided to have something to say about it. Kumar sneezed out a small cloud of white dust, after which Johnston insisted that he try again, but to do it slowly. This time, most of the magic medicine stayed inside Kumar. But before he could self-observe any effect on his own body, mind and soul, Johnston pulled his attention to something more important.

"Any new thoughts about Leona?" Johnston inquired.

"Thoughts about something more important are brewing between my ears now," Kumar replied, after which he tortured himself to a needed second look at the dam being built. The equipment being used was now so loud that he couldn't hear or feel Silence, that 'ringing' in the ears which he could always sense and connect to, even in the middle of a busy city street or wilderness thunderstorm. "What do we do about that dam damn?" Kumar grunted out as the structure got taller, and the river it was blocking got shallower.

"You're the director of this peoples' democracy," the former enforcer of all laws when Morgan owned Blue Water said to the present still somehow elected 'Civic Coordinator', as a compliment.

"Yeah…I am," Kumar replied, assertively, as if the soul of his grandfather, father and all of the grandfathers, fathers and unborn children of such in Blue River had cohabitated Johnston soul when he delivered that remark, and fact.

How Kumar would deal with the wish of being a Philosopher Comrade King that he never thought would happen was unknown to him. The REAL answer as to why he was now head of a community of individualists aspiring to think for themselves was as unknown as why the sky was blue. Why God created mosquitoes. And why a man and woman's idea of love were never the same thing. But he did know the 'where' the 'how' incubating in his soul, but not yet in his brain. It would have to be shared, and implemented, very soon.

CHAPTER 16

Kumar rode down the hill overlooking the dam towards town, noting the tributaries of the progressively drained and soon-to-be-completely-diverted river with every turn. Not showing up for the scheduled open town meeting to try to cooperatively, rather than oppressively, deal with the life-threatening water shortage would be disastrous. The urgency of such was all too apparent when he rode back to town, gazing at the dried beds of rock and dust which, just that morning, had been flowing streams of water. Clearly, a new plan was required. One that was bolder and more innovative than devising an ORDERED rather than voluntarily carried out rationing plan for whatever water was available.

Kumar felt his soul embracing what his brain now plotted out, awakened to the reality outside of his own head with the aid of Johnston's magic dust. The how-to-do-it was working itself out. The place where to formalize it would have to take place after sunset. Hopefully, with some cooperation from the ghost of sometime Wild West outlaw and sometime law-abiding citizen Sam Pickering.

It was a particularly warm, and yet another rainless, evening at the Old Hold Out where Kumar and Leona had shared, as well as designed, a plan to depose the rich and powerful without killing the innocent or the guilty. On the agenda for the scheduled town hall meeting was how to selectively, and safely, maintain Morgan and his horde of vicious Capitalist tyrants as passive, deluded puppets who would not interfere with the People's Revolution. How to still keep them as happy commoners who still didn't know who was cooking the drug and uranium-spiked food they enjoyed eating in selected 'holiday' mental hospitals.

Kumar, now turban-less, walked onto the podium with the 'all is well' upscale suit he wore in town a few days earlier to assure the public that the water situation very soon. He took to the podium at the Old Hold Out, which still had not fallen into the ground. He felt the absence of Leona as a Comrade and potential lover more than he expected, but he was somehow was not depressed by such. Rather he felt empowered. By perhaps the ghost of Sam saying that outlaws needed to trust each other. Or maybe the spirit of his grandfather Revolutionary Sikh making him feel like he was in control of his and everyone else's destiny, someone who didn't have to obey ANY rules anymore. Or maybe there was something in the powder which Johnston offered to him, confidentially, as such was in short supply, and needed to be used effectively, by the right people.

In any case, it was time for some serious Revolution rather than playful mischief. With the same rules of course. Make an impact but do no harm, since those who have the most guns, once the rules permitted them to be used, would surely demolish those who were less armed.

In front of Kumar was very selective company of citizens, chosen with the help of Johnston. The Sheriff Kumar had hated, feared and ridiculed most barely 4 months ago, over the past few days had become his now closest, and most trusted, advisor. The most innocent, vulnerable and perhaps most courageous of the citizenry Kumar was charged to serve in the meeting hall spoke up first.

"So, without water, what are we going to do about feeding our crops and animals?" Mary Steiner demanded, arms folded, her voice carrying both urgency and a broader compassion—for the people, for the animals, for survival itself. "And my children!" she added sharply, pulling her now eleven-year-old daughter into a tight, trembling embrace. Desperation, fear, and fury laced her tone— unapologetically fierce in her selective compassion.

"I'm not a child," Elsa muttered, wriggling out of her mother's embrace. She picked up her charcoal and resumed sketching notes about the meeting—not with words, but with images destined for the newspapers now and the history books later.

"And I belong to—"

"Yeah! The 'People's Revolution'!" Mary snapped, her face flushed beet red. "Which you keep telling me about," she added with a scornful grunt, then turned on Kumar, her fury erupting.

"The People's Revolution you keep telling her about! You don't even talk to me first because—"

"Because Elsa belongs to the Revolution," Kumar said firmly. But the voice wasn't entirely his—it came from somewhere deeper, more commanding. Someone else. Someone more forceful than the quiet thinker he usually was.

"Which is us," he added, turning to address the crowd—not as a comrade, but as something far more authoritarian. "All of us."

He inhaled deeply, trying to align the intensity in his chest with the clarity in his mind. Around him, the congregation passed around a canteen marked One sip only. DuBois took the first drink, then Buddy, then Jake—who passed it on without taking any. Dust clung to their faces. Their stubble bristled in the heat. Suspicion glinted in their tired eyes as they turned to Kumar.

Yet he kept speaking, feeling something surge up his spine and out of his mouth—a force shaking off the gentler soul he used to be.

"We all belong to the Revolution!" he proclaimed, suddenly seeing himself astride an invisible white horse. "Especially those who are digging wells and making the ground give us water!" The would-be cowboy, once an ally of nature, now challenged it.

"The ground isn't giving us water," Mary cut in. "Not enough, anyway…" Her voice cracked, mouth dry. She tried to go on, but the words stuck. After coughing several times—a sound Kumar observed evoked no sympathy in him—she met his gaze.

"You seem to have enough water to shave. And to keep that 'People's Mayor' suit clean and—"

Mary stopped mid-rant, startled by what Elsa was now drawing.

"What the hell—I mean heck—are you writing down now?" she shouted, a rare lapse in her usually measured tone. It was the first time anyone had heard her use that word in public.

"What fables are being immortalized as fact for the Revolution and the history books?!" She snatched the paper from under Elsa's small, ink-smudged hands.

"For our next article of people's liberation. For the world to read," Elsa replied calmly, unshaken. Her work, rich in both vocabulary and insight, had already outpaced her mother's understanding. "And a picture says a thousand words."

She pointed to a detailed charcoal sketch of Kumar.

"Words and pictures about a servant-director of the proletariat," Mary growled, showing it off to the others. "One who seems to be eating better than the rest of us."

The drawing portrayed Kumar as a robust hero—his belly full and the title A REAL Philosopher-Comrade for All the People beneath his name.

"That's not true! I'm not eating any better—or more—than any of you!" Kumar insisted, eyes darting toward the sketch. Ironically, it bore a strong resemblance to his grandfather.

"No, you're not stealing food from hungry people's tables," Jake chimed in, his voice sharp with sarcasm—a tone Kumar had never heard from the usually soft-spoken man. "You're just someone who needs a clear head, so he feeds his belly a little more. For the Revolution, of course."

"And with a little white powder up his nose," Buddy added, mimicking Jake's sarcasm as best his kind spirit could. "A honker that—"

"—Is receiving special medication," Johnston interrupted, standing abruptly as if the ground beneath him had become a podium. "For a special condition only he has. But if we go with the plan Comrade Kumar has—the one we've all been thinking but not saying—we get our water back. And whatever else we need."

"And that plan is what, Comrade King Kumar?" Mary demanded, louder and more piercing than anyone else. Every adult turned their eyes to him, pressing for an answer.

Kumar inhaled again—once for thought, once for courage. He gathered the tangle of secret, necessary actions into one stark truth.

"To kill or injure no one," he said.

"But to do severe damage," Elsa followed up, her voice soft but resolute. "Destruction to—" She handed her mother the newest sketch.

Mary looked down, then smiled. Proud. Relieved. Moved. She hugged Elsa tightly.

Elsa then held the drawing up for Kumar, and then the others to see—a quickly sketched image of the dam, destroyed.

Even Father Smith nodded.

"Alright, then. The details," Kumar said, wiping the sweat from his brow. He needed to see their faces clearly—those he would now trust with the plan.

CHAPTER 17

It was tradition in Jackson County—as in most counties on Colorado's western slope—to celebrate Easter with a bang. Old Man Winter never failed to leave everyone battered in one way or another. So Resurrection Day brought warmth, light, and gratitude. Winds carried a breath that no longer froze bare skin. Picnics, fireworks, and praise—spoken or unspoken—rose from the people, even from the Atheists. Fireworks weren't just welcomed. They were required. Easter brought more joy than Christmas or even the Fourth of July in these parts.

From the brush-covered overlook, Kumar scanned the completed dam through his binoculars. The once bold river had been swallowed into cracked mud under the oppressive Easter sun. On the dam's far side, the atmosphere was festive. Uniformed soldiers and well-dressed civilians picnicked behind rows of tanks and artillery, waiting for the command to invade Blue River.

A detachment of ten soldiers prepped the evening's fireworks, gulping from a shared jug between tasks. As in years past, the fireworks would begin as the sun slipped beneath the mountains.

Only three guards manned the bridge across the reservoir—eyes half-lidded, posture slack, rifles slung over their shoulders. They glanced with envy at the celebrants below.

"They don't seem worried about us," Kumar observed, lowering the binoculars. He glanced down at the Army uniform that clung to his body—and more dangerously, to the inflated sense of power surging through his drug-altered mind. "Who do they think we are? And who do they think I am?" he asked, half to himself.

"Someone who fits my Captain's uniform better than I did," Johnston replied, adjusting the homemade insignia on his own patched-up uniform. "But to pull this off, everyone in this People's Revolutionary Platoon needs to act the part."

Kumar followed Johnston's eyes to three unlikely saboteurs: Buddy, Jake, and DuBois. With Mary's help as makeup artist and costumer—a talent from her theater days—the men now resembled prim, respectable women. Wigs, corsets, dresses, and heels (painfully adjusted to accommodate their larger feet) transformed them into caricatures of ideal marriage prospects.

Buddy and DuBois frowned behind thick coats of red lipstick. But Jake—ever the rebel—walked proudly, exaggerated hips swaying, fake breasts jutting forward under a padded blouse. His picnic basket, like the others, was packed with treats for the guards—and sticks of dynamite strapped to their thighs beneath the skirts.

Dressed as a wealthy, overdressed young lady of ambiguous maternal origin, Elsa picked up her pencil and pad.

"No way Elsa's drawing me like this!" Buddy growled at Kumar, grabbing the sketchpad.

"Or me!" DuBois echoed, snatching the pencil.

"Mommy," Elsa said, turning sweetly to 'Mother' Jake, "tell your comrades I'm just drawing the women inside them. The ones stronger and smarter than the men they think they are. Right?"

Jake paused, lips trembling in an unfamiliar way. He smiled through freshly painted lips.

"Seems so," he replied, the former cowboy's voice gentle, even reflective. "Maybe... I hope," he added, his eyes cast downward, wrestling with something unexpected—and deeply human.

"That's enough wise cracking from you, still LITTLE girl," Dubois scolded Elsa in the same manner he did to his errand daughters at home. As Dubois saw it, Elsa needed a father who could stand up to her more than her mother did, or could. He grabbed Elsa by the waist and tied her to the wagon Mary had driven up the hill, next to her mother, who was already sitting on the buckboard. "Take both of these ladies home," he said to the mare hitched up to the harness. "No matter what any of them say."

"Why?" Elsa demanded of Kumar. "After I got all patriotic'd and Easter Sunday'd up for this?" she continued in a frightened convincing imitation of a pretty in pink Capitalist princess who loves her country as much as a father who steals hamburgers from the mouths of other kids so she can eat roast beef. "Why do I have to go home?"

Kumar had to think long and hard about his answer, as any flaw in his reply would be picked up and picked apart by the maiden who was sprouting extra brain cells 100 times faster than any of her girlfriends were sprouting breasts. "You have to go home because the Revolution needs some… innocence," he finally answered, after which he patted the horse on the ass and set it on his way, encouraged to not stop by Mary. "Alright, gentlemen, and ladies. You have your orders," Kumar announced to Johnston and the three 'ladies'.

"Your orders?!" Dubois barked back as an angry stallion and certainly not a gelding or a mare.

"Alright…then," Kumar replied, pulling his new personal backwards, and pushing his truer self into its place. "As not orders, but thought-infused requests that if not followed will fuck us all over. You okay with that?"

"Fer now," Buddy grumbled back. Jake nodded an affirmative 'yes'. Dubois moved away from Jake as if he were carrying a communicable disease. Johnston put his thumb up, enthusiastically, after which he opened up his left elbow, inviting Lady Jake to insert his arm under it. It left the management and difficulties of dealing with Mrs. Dubois and Miss Buddy to Kumar, according to the plan.

As the ensemble moved down the hill towards the dam, according to plan, Kumar heard, then saw, that Elsa had worked her way out of her restraints. She leaped out of her seat on the wagon and shot her sling shot at the ass of the horse, sending it and her mother back down the hill at a full gallop. As if being cohabited by the ghost of her slain Union Organizer father, she confidently marched to the overlook, took out her pencil and pad, and looked down below to record the events to happen. She helped herself to a full view of where the drama was to happen with a pair of her own, no doubt stolen, binoculars. Kumar thought about giving her another talk, but…he knew that someone had to survive what had to happen. Someone had to tell the world what was intended and what would occur. Truthfully, for a change.

CHAPTER 18

The corporal paced back and forth at his post on the bridge over the new reservoir—its water rights belonging to Smithmore County, Jackson's rival. When he saw Jake approaching, he averted his eyes, as if she embodied every woman he'd ever dreamed of marrying—and every girl back home he couldn't have.

Jake offered the young corporal, who sported only a peach-fuzz mustache, a sip from a flask of "liquid refreshment." But after sniffing the contents and realizing it held more alcohol than fruit, he declined—because he was on duty. Jake then extended an offer of specially spiced strawberry scones, which he also refused, citing "allergies."

Undeterred, Jake took a bite of a specially spiced hotdog, then offered the lonely—yet admittedly not bad-looking—corporal the chance to race her to the middle of the sausage. Just as the soldier leaned in to accept, his eyes glazed over. Then, they softened—enamored.

Captain Kumar arrived just in time, startling the corporal with an authoritative, "What are you doing with my wife, soldier!"—rescuing his "lady" from explorations that were far too early to begin.

The soldier snapped to attention as best he could. Kumar informed the sentry that he was just as entitled to celebrate the dam's completion as anyone else and ordered him to join his fellow guards below—who were enjoying the company of women who were, in fact, unattached. To drive the point home, Kumar took Jake by the hand and planted a kiss on her cheek.

"She lives to flirt with other men," he explained, "but that only makes her more lovable when she comes back to me."

The soldier accepted the reasoning and jogged off to join the festivities down below. Meanwhile, Kumar and Jake inserted sticks of dynamite—each with carefully timed long fuses—into the recesses of the concrete wall.

On the other side of the dam—the most vulnerable side—a potbellied sergeant patrolled the bridge. His ugly double chin and eyes permanently angry at the world made him appear more beast than man. Each stomp of his boots on the new bridge echoed like a five-story dinosaur trampling through the forest he perpetually claimed as his own.

Major Johnston approached, Miss Buddy draped on one arm and Lady Dubois on the other. Both women carried picnic baskets—one filled with tantalizing snacks, the other with dynamite hidden beneath skirts. In Buddy's case, her breasts seemed to change size with each seductive step.

The dinosaur sergeant marched up to the trio and raised his carbine rifle. "Who goes there!" he barked in a voice so deep it rattled the earlobes of everyone nearby.

Self-promoted Captain Johnston released the women from his arms and handed a note to the guard.

The sergeant's overgrown gray brows furrowed as he examined the note and peered into the baskets. His eyes squinted hard, trying to decipher the writing. Though he lowered his weapon, he didn't fully relax.

Johnston subtly pointed to the counterfeit insignias on his shoulders. "Captain," he reminded the sergeant.

Still suspicious, the sergeant continued reading. But Johnston knew that the quickest way to an overweight, duty-worn capitalist stooge was through his already overstuffed gut—especially when the food came spiced with mind-altering ingredients.

Dubois offered him a dazzling smile and a cookie crafted to delight his palate. He devoured it in a single bite. Buddy followed up with a generous slice of strudel. Without looking at either the pastry or its provider, the sergeant scarfed it down—a treat courtesy of master baker Mary Steiner and fledgling pharmacist Kumar.

Then, something shifted.

His bear-like torso swayed as though caught in a gust of hurricane-force wind, despite the still air. His eyes drooped halfway shut, though he remained upright, muttering complaints about his miserable, self-pitying life.

A crooked, drunkard's grin crept across his face as Buddy and Jake relieved him of his overcoat, cap, and rifle. They led him down toward the ongoing picnic, gently guiding him off the bridge. Johnston slipped into the sergeant's coat and cap, assuming his post like a seasoned actor stepping into a familiar role.

Discreetly, he removed the dynamite from the women's baskets—and from under their skirts—and motioned for them to leave the bridge with urgency, taking the sergeant with them.

Now alone, Johnston hid the sticks of dynamite in the exact spots dictated by Dubois—a self-taught builder forbidden from owning or even walking on the structures he once designed, all thanks to the "fat cats" who underpaid him.

Johnston—once a lawman serving the King, now a revolutionary burning with hatred for all things royal—glanced at the gold watch he'd received for his past "services" protecting Morgan and his ilk. Then he scanned all four directions, eyes thoughtful and calculating.

After a silent conversation with every corner of his mind, he slipped the watch beneath his tunic and retrieved a gold-plated lighter—pilfered from Morgan's overstocked closets. He struck it and lit the tip of a concealed fuse.

He checked his watch again.

Then looked up.

Two cars approached the bridge.

From each, a soldier stepped out—each with an all-American wife in tow, their futures already written in the form of yet-to-be-born all-American children. Following them was a man in a well-tailored brown vested suit, who removed his fedora to reveal—

The Foreman.

The very one who had whipped Johnston and his fellow prisoners in the chain gang, back when they were "honored" with the task of building the fence around Blue River during the infamous "sign-painting skirmish."

"Colonel Johnston! Happy Easter!" the first soldier called out, his voice full of cheer, abandonment, and ignorant glee.

"A celebration for us and our families," the second soldier added.

"Who…"

"…appreciate everything you've done for us," his impeccably dressed, well-fed wife chimed in, her smile gracing a goddess-like face—one that had likely never known blood, sweat, or tears. She followed her words with an aristocratic tilt of the head.

"After we… well, I didn't know you were working undercover," the first soldier said to Johnston, awkwardly apologetic.

"It was nothing personal. We… or rather, I… had to lay those lashes on your back while you were officially a prisoner," offered the former foreman of the chain gang, his voice teetering between guilt and deflection.

Johnston forced a thin smile of approval.

"In the service of…" the second soldier's wife continued, pointing to the diamond-studded American flag pin on her coat's lapel.

"And I hope you're still being paid handsomely by… them," the second soldier added, gesturing toward a black sedan pulling to a stop at the far end of the bridge.

From the vehicle emerged a plainclothes chauffeur and a nurse, escorting none other than the former moguls Ranselhoff and Younger. Though still dressed in their signature elegance—untouched by the hardships their decisions had caused—they now shuffled forward on weakened legs, their bodies barely supported by the same ground they once owned. Their eyes darted, wild and uncertain, like deer stumbling into a wolf's den, unsure if they were guests or prey.

"We're working on locating McDonald and the other CEOs," the second soldier explained, "and figuring out which Commie docs to bribe for their release. Oh, and brilliant move on your part—getting Kumar hooked on that special kind of cocaine. You know, the kind that gives you energy and pride at the expense of intelligence and common sense."

With smug glee, he reached into Johnston's breast pocket and pulled out a vial of white powder.

"Which will, eventually," Johnston began with a knowing smirk, "prove to these equality, fraternity, and liberty types that absolute power corrupts… absolutely." He plucked the vial back from the soldier's hand before he could sample its contents. "And that some of us," he continued, pocketing the drug, "are simply more powerful than others."

"And the rest of us are?" the other soldier asked. Not with fear, but with a calm curiosity, as if he already knew the answer and only wanted to hear Johnston say it.

Johnston took a long breath of twilight air, stroked his chin, and looked up at both men, his brothers-in-arms through countless campaigns overseas and at home, none of which would ever make the history books.

"You both, and so many others who take pleasure in being just like you," he said slowly, "are expendable. According to bosses you don't even know exist." He nodded toward Ranselhoff and Younger.

Before his former comrades could process the betrayal or react, Johnston drew two revolvers equipped with mini silencers from his holsters and aimed them squarely at the soldiers. The men didn't flinch. Their wives, however, attempted to slither away with their children.

"All of you—back here!" Johnston barked. The command halted their escape. "So you can get a full view of the fireworks," he added with a sneer.

One by one, Johnston lined up the soldiers and their families—children who had once called him "Uncle"—along the railing of the bridge overlooking the reservoir. Then, with brutal precision and a steady 4/4 rhythm, he hummed "The Battle Hymn of the Republic" and executed each of them. Their bodies slumped against the railing like lifeless mannequins in a grotesque display.

Two stanzas later, he turned his guns on Ranselhoff's nurse and Younger's chauffeur, sending them to whatever reward—or punishment—awaited them beyond a life of servitude.

With his final four bullets, Johnston shot Ranselhoff and Younger in both legs. They collapsed in agony, crawling pitifully away from the fast-burning fuse that now snaked toward the dam. Their cries for help were drowned out by the thunder of the first firework bursting overhead—a macabre prelude to a rural Colorado Easter spectacle that would rival any Fourth of July in Denver, Santa Fe, or Chicago.

Johnston escaped not sixty seconds before the charges detonated, the dam exploding in a brilliant flash before its creators could even realize it was gone.

As planned, Kumar, Dubois, Jake, and Buddy also made their getaway, riding off in a wagon driven by Mary

Steiner—disappearing just in time, the blaze lighting their retreat like a curtain closing on a stage.

The dried riverbed leading to Blue River flooded with water, welcoming the life-giving torrent with open arms. The concrete, wood, and steel used to build the dam were returned to the earth in chaotic disarray. But the bridge—upon which lay the dead bodies of two soldiers, their families, and two former moguls of industry along with their servants—remained eerily intact.

Angry and frightened men in blue, green, and black uniforms swarmed the site, assessing the damage. Photographers followed close behind, eager to capture snapshots of the so-called All-American Easter Celebration for the morning papers.

This is what Elsa saw—and sensed—from her post atop the hill, with eyes sharp as any hawk's, aided by super-powered binoculars; ears as attuned as any lead mare guarding a herd of foals; and lips capable of reading every whispered word, a skill she'd perfected during the year she'd gone functionally deaf.

She wondered why Kumar hadn't swung by to pick her up. But perhaps it was fate—some whisper from beyond—that told her she was meant to stay, to witness everything, and to report it to the world.

She remained there all night. Not because she was afraid to move, but because someone had to bear witness.

At the crack of dawn, Elsa watched the sun illuminate the mangled bodies of Ranselhoff and Younger as they were carried on stretchers toward an ambulance.

From seemingly nowhere, a portly, well-dressed man emerged. She recognized him instantly—Wentworth. With a subtle lift of his ring-heavy hand, he halted the stretcher-bearers. He knelt down, took the hands of the two slain men into his own, and kissed them both.

He made the sign of the cross three times over each of them, then laid a gold crucifix, a folded American flag, and a single flower upon their lifeless chests.

Photographers rushed in like moths to a flame, snapping pictures of the fallen men and the man blessing them. After wiping away a single tear, Wentworth rose to his feet and walked away from the crowd.

The ambulance—now plainly a hearse—took the bodies away, but not before Wentworth cast a glance up toward Elsa's hilltop post. Not directly—but directly enough.

His grief-stricken face transformed in an instant into a smug, shit-eating grin. The grin only widened as he was handed wanted posters, which were soon plastered along the bridge.

"Ten thousand dollars each. Reward. Dead or alive. For any of the murdering Anarchist Communist Terrorists," Elsa muttered, reading aloud to the rabbit that had wandered close for breakfast—ten feet from her at most.

She imagined it was her slain union activist father, reincarnated for one final conversation.

"A hefty sum for Kumar, Buddy, Jake, Dubois, Father Smith, and Mom—who all swore they would die before killing anyone else, Pop," she said softly. "But… interestingly… the same reward for 'Comrade Johnston,' who is wanted… alive."

"Which I am," came a man's voice behind her—half-whisper, half-wind.

She turned around, expecting to see a coyote possessed by her father's spirit, come for a post-mortem father-daughter heart-to-heart.

But no. It was something far more terrifying.

A man approached silently, extending a very human hand over her shoulder. He snatched the notebook she had filled with pages of observation and raw truth, then plucked the pencil she had worn down to a one-inch stump.

"The truth—as you see it, sense it—which is… astonishingly accurate," Johnston said as he skimmed her words and sketches. He spoke with an unsettling calm, more human than she had expected from a killer. "But…" he added, just as Elsa reached for her knife—aiming it straight at Johnston's oversized testicles.

In a flash, Johnston disarmed her, snatching the knife from her small hand. He pulled out his revolver and aimed it at her head.

She looked up. Unafraid.

She had lived more Alive, capital-A moments than any eleven-year-old girl she had ever known—perhaps even more than any one-hundred-year-old adult.

"Yeah. Yer right," Johnston said with a strange mix of admiration and pity.

He pulled a photo from his breast pocket—Elsa's mother.

From his Army General's holster, no less.

He held the revolver close to the picture.

"What do you want?" Elsa demanded.

"For you to, you know…" Johnston replied, beginning to tear pages from the manuscript Elsa had poured her blood, sweat, and tears into.

He handed the torn—but not destroyed—bundle back to her, motioning for her to finish the job herself.

Elsa froze.

What would her mother want her to do?

What would the Spirit—beyond any religion—require of her now?

And most urgently, what would Pop, who gave his life for the cause of workers now and in the future, expect of her?

She looked to the rabbit. It stared back at her, silent and waiting.

But before any message could be exchanged in a language she could understand, Johnston raised his revolver—and shot it.

The rabbit slumped, its life extinguished.

From the bushes above, as if summoned by heaven or hell, a crow swooped down and began pecking at the rabbit's body—starting with the eyes.

"That's the way it is," Johnston muttered. "The strong stay stronger. The virtuous become extinct."

He held up the photo of Mary once again.

"One more chance to do the right, patriotic, and Christian thing," he said. "And to keep doing the right, patriotic, and Christian thing."

With slow, trembling hands, Elsa tore up the rest of her manuscript—the best work she had ever done.

Her soul watched in agony as her hands destroyed what her heart had created.

Her mind, equally pained, envisioned a future where she would never write it again.

"Yes," Johnston said with a satisfied smile as the final pages scattered like confetti in the wind.

"Family before comrades. Smart choice."

He stroked Elsa's tear-covered cheek—tenderly, insultingly—before mounting his horse and riding back to town.

Elsa knew then—more painfully than ever—why selective compassion for family and friends can prevent someone from serving the world at full capacity.

And how not fighting oppression is itself a form of complicity.

Her days of being a theoretical genius were over.

Maybe, just maybe, if she became a good girl now and an obedient wife later, she could have a daughter—one brave enough to carry on the Revolution.

And more importantly, maybe Mary—Elsa's mother—could be that child's proud grandmother.

One who would justifiably encourage her granddaughter to never be the coward, or the fool, that Elsa had just become.

CHAPTER 19

The life-giving—and sometimes life-challenging—river flowed once again on its own terms, inviting two- and four-legged creatures alike to partake of its long-awaited return to Blue River and the rest of Jackson County. But its revival came at a steep cost. The rules of the "game" had changed—and it was no game anymore.

Blue River, once a haven without fences or barriers to any who wished to enter or leave, had become a fortress. Unused wagons and every plank of lumber not vital to shelter were repurposed into barricades. Books were torn apart and converted into cartridges for double-barreled muskets and Kentucky long rifles, retrieved from mantels and the dusty archives of the Homestead Museum. Whether such makeshift defenses could hold against the tanks now encircling the town was another story entirely.

But one story hit Kumar harder than most. It arrived in the form of a newspaper smuggled past the blockade—whether by courage or connivance, no one could say. "Pacifist People's Revolutionaries Become Murderous Terrorists" blared the headline in the New York Herald

Gazette—the very publication that, until now, had boosted morale in Blue River with Elsa Steiner's impassioned dispatches, winning over Eastern readers with tales of a dream still alive out West.

There was, however, one truth in that bitter ink: every citizen who remained in Blue River was now armed with something capable of tearing open flesh or ending a life.

Kumar, whose ceremonial Sikh knife had once symbolized spiritual honor, now wore Colt revolvers on both hips and slung a Winchester rifle across his shoulder. As he stood helping to reinforce the barricades, Jake, Buddy, and Dubois organized the defensive militia with synchronized efficiency, three men thinking and acting as one. They passed along the hopeful fiction that U.S. soldiers and private militia hired by Wentworth and company would not fire if Blue River's citizens held firm—to their weapons, their senses, and their nerves.

Among those defenders stood, quite unbelievably, Morgan and Richter—the moguls reborn. Hospital staff insisted they had enlisted voluntarily. Dressed in denim overalls and cowboy jeans, the two former titans of industry now struggled to operate the only weapons deemed safe for them: slingshots. With childlike determination and fogged minds—but oddly light spirits—they managed to tangle themselves in the elastic bands until Mary, now affectionately referred to as "Duchess" by some, rushed over.

"No, Sir Morgan... and Sir Richter," she said gently, untangling the bands from their wrists, arms, and—just in time—their necks. Once free of their elastic entrapments, Mary blinked at the devices, puzzled by the modifications Elsa had made. She called her daughter over.

Elsa arrived promptly—surprisingly silent, without a hint of her usual wit or commentary about adult incompetence.

"Is something wrong?" Mary asked gently. Again.

Elsa said nothing. Her answer came in the form of action. She took the slingshots in her hands and, with sudden fury, snapped them apart, breaking the weapons and channeling her rage into the splintered wood and rubber. Then, with downcast eyes and silent feet, she slithered away without a word.

"Do I know her?" Morgan asked, raising a bushy, puzzled eyebrow.

"I think we did," Richter added, scratching his head. "When we were… who were we?"

"Rich men who became poor ones," Mary heard a voice say behind her. It was Melissa, her once-dismissed fellow sister-in-struggle, now clad proudly in militia garb. A red star gleamed on the headband across her brow, her chest defiant, her stance unyielding.

"You were rich men who became poor ones, then patients who—"

Mary's sharp look cut Melissa off before she could push further, reminding the men who they had once been, and who they never would be again—not if Mary had anything to say about it. Morgan and Richter slumped back into their odd stupor: content, peaceful, and confused.

But Melissa's mood quickly shifted when Kumar approached—newly turbaned and weighed down with weapons and sorrow.

"Yes," Melissa continued, her tone now soft and reverent. "Rich men who became poor ones, then patients who—"

"—Will be, somehow, treated," Kumar interrupted. His voice was low, thoughtful. The Commander of a doomed dream.

Melissa wrapped her blistered yet still delicate fingers around his arm. "So they can become real people again."

"Moron Morgan and Ratshit Richter were never real people, or men," she added, a spark of the old fire still lingering. "Not like you, Kumar. You converted me. You made me dedicated to something bigger than myself." Her voice cracked, then steadied. "Thank you."

Kumar smiled, a tired, sad smile. Maybe this was his greatest victory: the transformation of a greedy, cunning, status-hungry woman into someone who gave more than she took.

"I am dedicated to something bigger than all of us!" Melissa shouted to the crowd with a raised fist, her voice echoing through the chilled spring air. "Power to the people!"

The barricade builders couldn't resist. They joined in, repeating the chant—not just to affirm their beliefs, but to muffle their fears. Power to the people! they cried, until the hills rang with the roar of defiance.

But Kumar felt no triumph—only dread. To him, the chant sounded hollow, the fire of revolution reduced to smoke and sound. The people were determined. And the people were doomed.

Comrade Johnston entered the square on horseback, his steed burdened with crates of unmarked ammunition. Under the chorus of "Power to the people," Kumar thought he heard Johnston mutter something else: Power to the idiots. It wasn't just the sound—it was the shape of the lips. Kumar's sharp eyes caught it.

He didn't have time to confirm it.

A new sound emerged from beyond the line of tanks—a grinding, mechanical roar that seemed to tear through the bones of the earth. It wasn't a tank. It was worse. It was the sound of something unfamiliar, unnatural. A motorized specter.

And Kumar knew in his trembling bones: this was no ordinary arrival.

This… was a visitor from hell.

Or worse.

A special envoy from Washington.

"Shut up!" Kumar bellowed to the enthusiastic crowd, uncaring if he came across as a buzzkill, a party pooper, or the deflator of much-needed morale.

"Shut the fuck up!" he repeated, louder and more urgent.

The chant died out. Silence rippled through the barricades as he pressed his binoculars into his bloodshot eye sockets, scanning the eastern horizon.

An open jeep, weaving through the wall of tanks and artillery, finally parked on the high ground visible to every naked eye in town. In it sat Major Sam Longmore and his superior, Colonel Daniels. Sam, now donning the authority of a full officer, took a bullhorn from a subordinate and held it like he'd been born with it in his hand.

"Everything goes back to normal," he began, his voice eerily similar to the cowboy, rancher, and horse trainer he'd been before uranium therapy rewired his soul, "if you give us the saboteurs who blew up the dam and killed two families."

He paused for effect, then raised his voice.

"They killed six innocent people!"

He gestured toward a billboard just erected by defectors—two civilians from the neighboring county and three ex-Blue River residents. On it were printed the faces of two common soldiers, two military wives, and two children. All lost in the blast.

"Six innocent people. Murdered."

Kumar and his fellow holdouts said nothing. They did even less—until Daniels seized the bullhorn from Sam's hand.

"EIGHT innocent people!" he thundered.

Another team of defectors moved into view, this time unveiling towering portraits of slain business moguls Ranselhoff and Younger—smiling paternalistically down at the town that had betrayed them.

Crack. Crack. Crack.

Three gunshots rang out.

Two of the bullets struck the businessmen's likenesses squarely between their digitally retouched eyes. The third knocked the hat clean off Daniels' head.

"Who fired those shots?" he roared, hurriedly sweeping the long strands of hair from one side of his head to cover the near-bald dome at the top.

"WHO FIRED THOSE SHOTS?"

Jake raised his hand.

Two other militia members raised theirs after a pause no longer than two heartbeats. Then a dozen more followed.

Melissa, not to be outdone, scrambled onto a heap of scorched lumber, raising her arm high for all sides to see—especially Kumar.

"Until we find out who did this," Daniels growled as an aide returned his shredded hat, "and this," he added, gesturing toward the display of dead victims, "nobody comes out. And nobody gets in!"

Kumar's ears pricked up again. Something was coming from the tree-lined southern edge of town. He saw the birds take flight before he heard the roar. Another motorized vehicle—bashing its way through the bush.

He snatched up his binoculars again, ignoring the warmth of Melissa's arms wrapped around his sweat-soaked waist—whether loving or manipulative, he couldn't say.

When he saw it, he knew.

"LET THIS ONE THROUGH!" Kumar shouted to the crowd.

The truck emerged like a wounded beast—bullet-riddled, lurching on three and a half defiant wheels, carving its own road through the foliage.

"Give him cover—NOW!"

Kumar ripped himself from Melissa's embrace as his comrades opened fire—not on the truck, but on the tanks and machine nests now targeting it.

The battered vehicle pushed forward as long as it could, until its axle shattered and it collapsed in the town square. The engine let out a strangled puff of smoke before dying. Radiator fluid and oil puddled beneath it like blood beneath a fallen soldier.

"Made in America," said Doc Wilson as he hobbled out through the shattered windshield, "destroyed by America."

He added, with a bittersweet grin, "Along with most—but not all—of what's in the back."

The man who had saved so many lives—yet, as far as Kumar knew, never taken one—limped to the rear. With grim pride, he yanked the mangled rear door from its hinges, ducking just in time to avoid losing his one good leg.

Citizen comrades surged forward, hauling out intact crates of medical supplies, food, and weapons that Wilson had "confiscated" during his so-called medical conference in Fort Collins and other places he refused to name.

Kumar searched the crates, his eyes hunting for something else.

"Got any of this, Doc?" he asked, pulling Wilson aside and showing him a small vial of white powder—his last dose of the special compound Doc Johnston had prescribed for Kumar's…unique physiology.

"Your special recipe," Kumar whispered, pressing the vial into Wilson's hand. "You know—the one that makes good men into effective ones."

Wilson sniffed it. Tasted it. Frowned.

Morgan and Richter passed behind them, each armed with slingshots and busy using them…on themselves.

"I'm a piece of shit and garbage," Morgan sang in a flat, discordant moan that tugged on Kumar's shame.

"And I should die," Richter croaked.

Kumar winced. The words hit too close.

He turned back to Wilson.

"So, as I was saying…" he said under his breath, "I need more. Of that."

Wilson's face hardened.

"That's not in my cookbook. And it's not on my clinic shelves either," he said, after one more taste. "Where did you get this?"

Kumar pointed toward Johnston, who was now arming children—no older than ten—with handguns and rifles. Elsa tried to stop him, tugging weapons out of the small arms of her former classmates—the same ones who had bullied and mocked her.

But when Johnston looked at her, she froze.

After he turned away, she resumed her quiet resistance—placing repeater rifles back into the hands of children barely bigger than the guns they carried.

Kumar observed himself—his mind issuing commands to his confused, pharmacologically altered brain to see what had always been in front of his eyes… yet had somehow escaped them.

From his pocket, he pulled out a copy of the wanted poster—featuring himself and three of his comrades—one of the hundreds scattered across the town square just an hour earlier. Something flickered in what remained of his fractured cognition.

"The only one on this wanted poster who's listed as wanted alive, and not dead, is Johnston," he finally realized aloud.

He glanced toward Elsa—who, Kumar now noticed, would confiscate weapons from the armed and determined teenage fighters whenever Johnston looked her way, only to quietly return them once he turned his back.

"And every time Comrade Johnston looks at Elsa," Kumar muttered, "she turns into…"

"Someone she isn't," Wilson finished, his voice low.

"And won't be again," Kumar growled, crumpling the wanted poster in his fist—anger directed more at himself than anyone else. But first, he was determined to settle the score with Johnston.

"And… some pictures I came across in Fort Collins," Wilson added, stepping closer. "When I tried to console the families of the dead soldiers… medically, anyway."

He pressed his left hand to Kumar's trembling chest and discreetly slid a set of photographs into view. Kumar's bloodshot eyes narrowed as he focused.

"Cameras don't lie. Not yet anyway," Wilson said, his voice flat. The photos showed 'Uncle' Johnston at an anniversary party—with the two slain soldiers, their wives, and their children. According to the ribbon behind them, the photo had been taken three days before the dam was blown up.

"Take care of this situation with this," Wilson said, tapping Kumar's head. "Not this toxic, powdered firewater."

He reached into Kumar's pocket and pulled out the nearly empty vial of the specially formulated cocaine that Doc Johnston had prescribed for 'Philosopher King sucker Kumar.' He tossed it into the dirt.

"And not that either," he added, pointing to Kumar's clenched fist, so tightly balled that blood now dripped from his palm.

"In the battle between intelligence and power, the winner will always be—"

"Whoever we say it is," Kumar grunted.

With that, he shoved the good doctor aside and marched toward Johnston.

The double-agent turncoat—'Comrade' Johnston—was in the process of handing a vintage .45 caliber buffalo rifle from the Heritage Museum to a boy barely nine years old, half the weapon's size. He offered it as casually as a toy from Santa Claus. A toy that Kumar knew was defective—if fired, the barrel would dislodge, sending shrapnel not at the target, but directly into the person holding the trigger.

"You're never too young to fight," Johnston said, his voice coated in deceptive warmth. His latest 'expendable' soul was none other than Gullible Geoffrey—always eager to believe any tale of heroism told to him by anyone, except the ones that mattered most, the ones his own father never got the chance to tell—before dying an ugly and unnecessary death fighting the Kaiser.

"Never too young to fight, and if necessary, die for what's Right," Johnston proclaimed.

"Or too late to correct what's wrong," Kumar interjected calmly.

For reasons he couldn't yet explain, he reached into his jacket and silently showed Johnston the photos Wilson had handed him.

"They were… friends," Johnston replied after what seemed to be a pause of genuine reflection and pain. "Friends who turned on me."

"In a picture taken days before they were blown up," Kumar pointed out coldly.

"By... accident!" Johnston snapped. "Because they were on the wrong side."

He turned toward Elsa, reaching out to gently pull her close.

"Comrade Patel. Kumar. Ask your—no, our—brilliant, honorable, and beautiful historian. She'll tell you the truth."

Johnston looked down at Elsa with a tenderness that startled everyone present. It was the kindest tone Kumar—or anyone in town—had ever heard come from Johnston's lips.

"Tell them the truth, Elsa," he said softly. "I'm one of you now... right?"

Elsa looked up at him, her face twisted in fear and fury.

Kumar turned his back on her, pretending to cough.

But in the reflection of his lighter—the one Sam had given him—he saw everything.

The wink.

The flash of a photo—Elsa's mother.

And Johnston's fingers slicing across his own throat in a silent warning: Defy me again, and she becomes an orphan.

"I… yes. Yes," Elsa stammered, her voice trembling. "You're one of us now."

"Sure," Kumar said, his voice flat. "If you say so, Elsa."

He turned away. "I'll just go back to what I was doing, while you and Comrade Uncle Johnston—"

Before Johnston could reach for his gun—or unleash another bullet made of lies—Kumar lunged. He grabbed Johnston by the bandana and the two men struggled, bodies colliding as the whole town watched in stunned silence.

Wilson, being a foot shorter than most of the surrounding crowd, couldn't see what was happening. He shoved his way through, trying to reach them.

But Johnston emerged from the tangle—with Kumar's gun. He seized Elsa by the hair, dragging her toward him as he raised the barrel to her head.

"Guns down, you deluded idiots!" Johnston roared. His voice dropped into the harsh, deep tone of the sheriff he used to be—one who never bluffed, and who always walked away the last man standing.

"This town will belong to the people who built it—and who will rebuild it in America's image, not yours. So help me, God!"

And to prove to the newcomers—those who didn't yet understand what "So help me, God" had meant in the 'good old days'—he shot Elsa in the left foot.

Screams erupted.

"The next one goes into her brilliant, subversive, demonic Communist head," he snarled.

"So help me God," he repeated, looking up at the sky.

Mary Steiner, Elsa's mother, rushed forward to rescue her daughter. But from the corner of his eye, Johnston turned and fired. The bullet struck Mary in the exact same spot on her foot where her daughter had just been hit. Then, without hesitation, he fired again—this time into her knee—crippling her advance.

Every gun in town rose in unison, aimed squarely at Johnston.

"Lower them!" he barked. "All of you. Or mother and daughter get matching shots in the organ they value most."

He moved his revolver back and forth—hovering between Elsa's overly developed brain and Mary's heart. Elsa screamed "No!" each time he aimed at her mother. Mary did the same when the weapon turned toward Elsa.

Kumar slowly lowered his gun, setting it gently on the ground. Then he raised his hand and motioned for everyone else to do the same. One by one, reluctantly, they obeyed.

"I'm taking these two with me," Johnston announced. "Insurance."

Kumar stepped forward, arms raised. "Take me instead. I'm—"

"—the one who will surrender this revolution. To me. Now!" Johnston interrupted coolly, grabbing a Tommy gun with enough ammunition to mow down twenty revolutionaries before they could say Internationale.

"I'm the new boss," he declared with the same smugness Morgan and Richter had once worn like crowns when they ruled the town—and him.

"No," Kumar dared to say, his voice steady despite the weight of fear and fury in the air. "No, you're not the new boss."

"Yes, I am the boss of this town!" Johnston yelled at the hushed crowd. "A town that won't be fucked over by other bosses who are now losers!" He turned to Morgan and Richter, waking them from their stupefied silence. "Losers whose fiancée and mistress I fucked again and again under the sheets! And she liked it!" he roared, eyes gleaming with cruelty. "Right, Madam Melissa?"

"No!" Melissa shouted, eyes full of shame, staring at a heartbroken Richter and a furious Morgan. "Not true!"

"Oh yes," Johnston grinned savagely.

Melissa curled into herself, overcome with shame as Johnston went on—detailing, loudly and lewdly, every way he had degraded her, all while plotting the financial ruin of the two men who once fought for her love.

But Johnston hadn't finished.

"And you, Comrade Kumar," he said, eyes narrowed on the philosopher-jokester who had long mocked him. "Sing—yes, sing—to these so-called educated rebels. Tell them they're garbage. That they should die. Say it!"

"No," came a voice from behind Johnston. Not Kumar's. It was Richter.

He and Morgan had somehow managed to merge their broken slingshots into a single, functional weapon. They fired a stone that struck Johnston square in the back, knocking him off balance—and knocking the Tommy gun from his hands.

As the crowd gasped, Elsa seized the moment. She delivered a fierce kick straight into Johnston's groin, sending him crumpling to the ground.

Johnston doubled over, eyes clenched shut in agony. When he opened them again, he was met with a hail of bullets tearing into his chest.

He looked up one last time—and saw the face of his executioner.

"For my dead husband. Who lives again," said Mary Steiner, calm and resolute, in both English and German. She stood firm behind the stock of the Tommy gun he had dropped.

"And who lives in us," she added.

She raised the gun and fired again—this time into Johnston's skull. His nearly headless body collapsed to the earth.

And then, with a voice steady and sure, Mary began singing The Internationale. One by one, voices joined her—Morgan, Richter, Melissa, and finally, even Kumar, his voice off-key but full of spirit.

Then came another voice. Clear. Deep. Unmistakable.

Sam Longmore was walking into town, alone. His rich, operatic baritone—known for calming skittish cattle and settling barroom disputes—rose above the others.

"There's been enough killing—by accident and on purpose," said Sam, now standing before them all. He stripped off his guns and threw them to the ground. "Too much rendering unto Caesar."

"And not enough rendering unto God that which is God's," Kumar added, something stirring deep within him, sparked by the quiet conviction in Sam's eyes. He dropped his weapons too and folded his hands in prayer.

"Hey, get back here, Captain Longmore!" Daniels shouted from the barricade. "I can still promote you to Major!"

"Private would be better," Sam replied, peeling off his insignia.

"Or convict," Daniels countered, raising his rifle. "You're under arrest."

"Liberated convict," Sam said calmly, "surrendering to a higher court than yours, Colonel."

He walked forward with one hand holding a white flag. In the other, he carried two letters. He handed one to Kumar, who unfolded the envelope addressed to him.

"There's information in there," Sam said, "about them"—nodding toward the well-armed soldiers behind him.

Kumar read the letter carefully. Around him, revolutionaries kept their guns raised, staring down the military forces that surrounded them. Those soldiers stared back, equally tense.

Finally, Kumar finished reading.

"So why is this addressed to me—and one other person only?" he asked Sam.

"Because power corrupts absolutely, and no one, including me, knows what's going to happen today. And that includes them also," Sam said as he pointed to the East, West, and South horizons, beyond the army trucks, tanks, and artillery. "Spears and arrows against tanks," Sam continued. Kumar beheld more armed to the teeth with anything they could carry or put on a saddle, Indians than he had ever seen in full traditional regalia, led by Chief Russell and Leona. "The Indians coming in to save your Palefaces from my Palefaces," Sam added.

The soldiers caught between the Indians and the Paleface Revolutionaries aimed their weapons at the one or the other 'adversary', each man seeming to decide which of them he had a chance of stopping.

"And all of this being watched by----" Sam pointed to the Northern horizon.

"---Reporters who…work for who?" Kumar inquired about the number of cars stopping at the Northernmost overlook. Men, and even a few women, with fedoras, flash cameras, movie cameras, portable microphones, and notepads emerged from the vehicles, lining up to record what was to happen below.

"Them I didn't expect," Sam said regarding the press. "Not yet anyway…"

"So," Kumar asked his newest ally, and re-found friend. "What do I do now. Or…what do WE do no?"

That most critical explanation from Sam's lips which Kumar wanted and needed to hear was silenced by a thunderous blast from Daniels' long-range rifle that landed between Sam's open ears. Daniels then aimed his rifle at Kumar's head. Kumar prepared for his final reward, or next incarnation. But, alas, he was sentenced to life by an arrow that went straight into Daniel's head, released from Leona's bow.

Daniels' third-in-command, a young First Lieutenant, looked at the arrow, then at the situation, and ran his fingers through his thick hair.

"We go, and no one gets scalped. Deal?" he yelled up to Leona.

She turned to Chief Russell, who flipped a coin into the air.

"Heads or tails?" Leona asked the Lieutenant.

"Heads?" the terrified junior officer replied.

"Tails, future baldies," Chief Russell called back to the soldiers. He motioned for his horde of riders, drivers, and infantry "Injuns" to head home. The soldiers dispersed—after the Indians did—in different directions. For now, anyway.

The cameramen remained where they were, capturing whatever footage they could from a VERY, VERY safe distance.

Kumar looked down at his slain friend. Sam's now-lifeless fingers still held the second letter he had brought. Father Paul gave Sam his last rites—a benediction heard and absorbed by everyone present… except the person named on the letter.

Kumar gently took it from Sam's hand and walked toward Elsa, who had separated herself from the crowd of fighters-turned-mourners.

"Something you want to give me—or tell me?" Elsa asked, her voice steady, her tone that of a woman hardened by life, educated more by what is than by what should be.

"For when you're... younger again," Kumar said softly. Then he pocketed the letter.

When the benediction ended, Kumar turned to the still-partially-armed populace, rolled up his sleeves, and began dismantling the barricade.

"Each gives according to their abilities, and takes according to their needs. For as long as we can."

CHAPTER 20

1968. Hollywood, Los(T) Angeles.

An old-in-body but defiantly young-in-spirit woman sat across from two bell-bottom-suit-trousered executives, each half her age with a hundred times more wealth and connections.

The manuscript she had written—sixty years defiant and still pulsing with life—lay on their desk.

"So... what was written in that letter, Ms. Steiner?" the first producer asked, the kind who claimed to be "working within the system to change it." He leaned back in his easy chair, stroking his manicured fingers through a perfectly symmetrical $300 "hippie working man's" hairdo.

"A message from Leona to Kumar? Elsa?" asked the slightly older, maybe wiser associate producer, scratching a freshly grown goatee as if trying to draw attention away from the thinning hair on top of his head.

"What happened to Blue River?" the younger gatekeeper pressed, the one standing between artists and the people who needed to hear what they had to say.

"It held on. For a while anyway. On its own terms. Long enough to make a statement. To keep the Revolution alive for future generations. Which is… you. And your kids," Elsa replied. "As you may have—or I hope—read in the script I just put on your desk."

"Which you've been marketing for the last 25 years. With no success, apparently," the older producer noted flatly. "Along with yourself as a writer, I see from your résumé. What happened?"

"Another blacklist at home. Another war in Europe. Then another blacklist at home after we 'won' the war in Europe," Elsa answered from a chest and mouth that had survived two bouts of mysteriously occurring cancers and two "accidental" beatings—one in jail, the other in a mental hospital, where she'd been diverted by the second judge she had dared to challenge while defending a city of broke-but-not-poor people against a corporation that wanted to own their town—and their souls.

"But it's part of the cycle, which has its own clock," she added. "Our isolated and historically unrecorded revolution in the dirty thirties paved the way for the hip, cool, popular, and very marketable revolution now. Which I hope is going to be about more than sex, drugs, and rock and roll."

"We don't call it 'rock and roll' anymore," the younger gatekeeper said, smugly dismissive of hard-earned wisdom.

"But your script... it does have some relevance," he added, "and I think, a market now. But—we'll have to make some changes in the narrative, of course. To increase popularity, appeal—"

"—And sales. I know," Elsa cut in, holding onto as much courtesy as she could manage beneath the storm of rage rising inside her.

She looked at the two young capitalist gatekeepers, watching them fool both the world and themselves into thinking they were integral members of the "don't trust anyone over thirty" generation. She wondered if they were ready for one more dose of truth from an old dinosaur.

But as her doctor—none other than Jake—had said, she would join Kumar in the Happy Hunting Grounds in six months or less. And maybe, just maybe, there was some functional justice—or at least a reason—why one could be rich in vision but not in pocket.

She had to say it. "Without fuckhead, manipulative, bastard, motherfucker tyrants and pseudo-liberal capitalists like you," she said to the committee of "hip, too-cool-to-sweat" elitists across the table, "true, honest, and intelligent revolutionaries would be out of work—and Purpose."

"Like the fuckhead, manipulative bastard motherfucker bosses Sam Longmore listed? The ones he gave to Kumar? Which he gave to you?" one of the producers asked.

"Which I inherited from him," Elsa said, her voice breaking ever so slightly. "After he, well… died a noble death trying to bring them down too fast."

She paused, gathered herself.

"But—gotta die of something, right?"

"A 'B-line' from a B-movie," the younger gatekeeper smirked.

"But it's true," his older colleague conceded.

"And it can become hip again—if spoken by a really cool, groovy, happening, right-on actor or actress," Elsa added, using the very metaphors she had satirized with intelligence and depth across her unpublished books and small-audience radio shows.

"What's old always becomes new again," she continued. "Part of the cycle. And if we push hard enough, it might just lead us upward—instead of spinning around in dead-end circles."

The words spilled out of her from a place she couldn't name—but could feel. She looked at the table separating them from us, almost wanting to thank the third mind that had just entered the room, even if—so far as she could tell— there was only one expansive, functioning brain present.

Then, something groovy happened.

The ghost of Kumar—or some other expression of Spirit (big S), as he always called it—made itself known.

"We'll take this upstairs to our bosses," the first wet-behind-the-ears executive offered, holding Elsa's true-life story, now transformed into both novel and script.

"And if they don't like it—to their bosses," the elder gatekeeper promised, rising from his chair and extending a hand.

"We'll be in touch." His handshake felt firm. And honest.

Elsa walked out of the office not knowing, of course, whether the bosses on top would greenlight it. But she was convinced—somehow—that if they didn't, she could rally enough people at the bottom to make something happen. On the big screen. In the theaters. On the small screens at home.

Or maybe the few people who still read would buy a book from an author who was also a publisher. Or maybe—just maybe—there would someday be a way to distribute truly independent works. No gatekeepers. Just words. Stories. Pictures. Shared across airwaves. Free. Accessible. Worldwide.

Something to call... perhaps... the internet.

ABOUT THE AUTHOR

MJ Politis departed the womb in Hoboken, New Jersey, in 1951.

To make good on what everyone who supported, taught and challenged him did, he obtained a Ph.D. in physiology in 1978 which was used to publish 46 research papers in medical journals in reconstructive neurology, toxicology and cancer treatment.

He went on to obtain a veterinary degree to extend medical care to fur bearing souls in a wide variety of clinics and cultural settings across the US and Canada. In order to diagnose and cure numerous maladies of the human soul, he obtained an H.B.A.R.P. degree (human being, aspiring Renaissance person) as author of over 80 novels and novellas, as well as producer/director/writer on 27 comedo-dramatic films, which can be accessed through:

www.longriderpress.net.

He has been owned by horses for the last 40 years, currently residing in Interior British Columbia, Canada as home base, regularly commuting to New York to maintain global perspective.

Reach out to me at:

<u>mjpolitis@yahoo.com</u>